W9-DGJ-180

BY SHERRIL JAFFE

Scars Make Your Body More Interesting (1975)
This Flower Only Blooms Every Hundred Years (1979)
The Unexamined Wife (1983)

sherril jaffe

The Unexamined Wife

black sparrow press
santa barbara · 1983

 For information address Black Sparrow Press, P.O. Box 3993, Santa Barbara, CA 93105.

LIBRARY OF CONGRESS CATALOGING IN PUBLICATION DATA

Jaffe, Sherril, 1945-
The unexamined wife.

I. Title.
PS3560.A314U5 1983 813'.54 83-11915
ISBN 0-87685-570-2
ISBN 0-87685-571-0 (signed)
ISBN 0-87685-569-9 (pbk.)

For my dear Alan

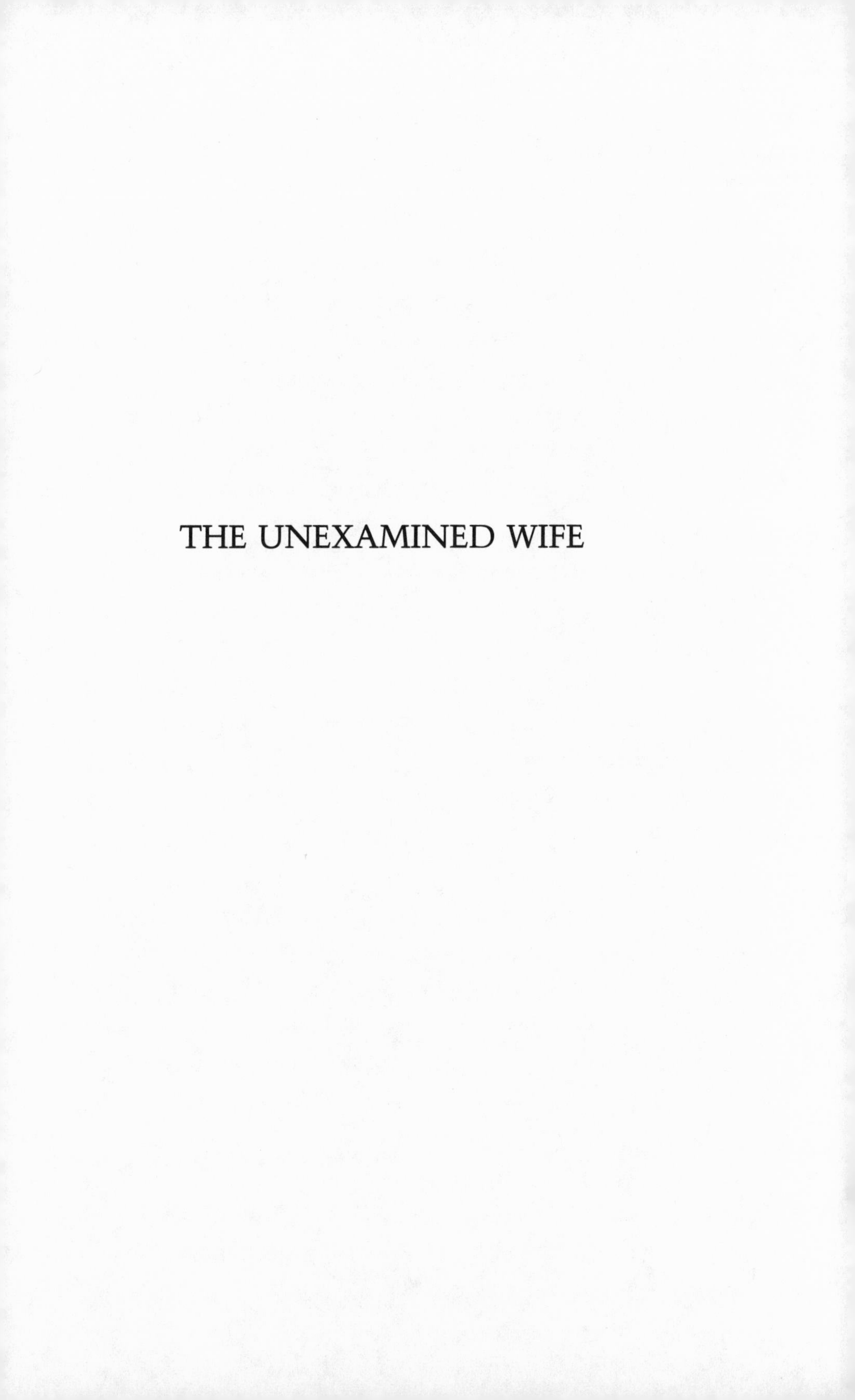

THE UNEXAMINED WIFE

Part 1

The Unexamined Wife

A Wedding in the Country

FROM HIGH UP, from above, where the sounds are indistinct, so that they sound like babble, although it could be Italian, is a clear view of the table, though it is unclear who is eating, or the reason for the celebration, which from this distance looks like any Italian country wedding, though, if you raise your eyes even further, you can see out beyond the distant hills through a fissure in the landscape, beyond the rim of the world. And now, winding away from the whole proceeding, is the small car of the judge.

This was Ann's wedding party. She wondered if it was significant that there were thirteen at table.

But she and Ben hadn't wanted a large wedding. This wedding was just for show. For, in fact, she was sure she already felt married while they were just living together, and that this simple ceremony was just to appease the world, or, more specifically, her parents, who wanted her to be happy. So she had gone out one day and bought herself this wedding dress, which was actually an off-white mini-dress, rather cheap, for she would never wear it again, and ordered these flowers, for it was fall, and no flowers were blooming, and together she and Ben had bought this ring for ten dollars. She had insisted on real gold, though Ben had told her just to go down to the dime store and pick out anything.

They were not materialists, after all. Nor did they care for surfaces, only essences. Still, this day was dedicated to appearances, so before leaving the house to spend her last few days under her father's name Ann had been careful to dust and wax the table. Then, on top of it, she had placed a large plastic cloth to protect it and keep the dust off till she got there right before the ceremony with Mother and Father in a rented car. All Ben had to do was remove the plastic right before they arrived.

They were late. Ben had forgotten. He didn't see plastic.

During the night, the gold hills had blown to dull dried weeds. The outline of the mountains had been rubbed out by haze. Now they had all entered the house which Ann had never before seen imperfect, champagne on plastic. Father was snapping pictures. People wondered what to say, and Mother laughed, her bright face framed against the window against which a thousand flies clustered and buzzed, waiting to penetrate.

Although it was not a particularly spectacular fuck, Ann was glad that she and Ben made love that night, officially their wedding night, and yet a night like any other. They were not going on a honeymoon; they were already there—in paradise—and never had to go anywhere anymore.

Vacuum Cleaner Salesman

THERE WAS A MAN on the phone mispronouncing her name. Ann was alone in the house, and the wind was blowing all around. Ben was working late at the office. Yet now she *was* Mrs. So-and-So, like a woman in a book.

He was offering her something. Perhaps the answer to all her dreams, the cure for all her fears—absolutely free—all she had to submit to was a simple demonstration. She had always hung up on people like this in the past. But what had she known? She would have it done while Ben was working late at the office.

Ann's living room and dining room were attached. Did this mean they were one room or two?

Two. But it was all one rug.

What if she had just had one half of the rug cleaned, then, by this special method?

Certainly, that would be possible, Mrs. So-and-So, but if one half of the rug was clean and the other half wasn't, then the side which wasn't clean would really stick out. It would look really dirty. It would be an entirely different color.

"It's not my fault!" Ann pleaded. "It's the fault of the woman before me!"

"Of course it's not your fault, Mrs. So-and-So," the vacuum cleaner salesman said. "Now how about that free demonstration?"

"Oh, thank you!" Ann said, prepared not to buy anything.

First he opened it up and extended its parts. He showed her how it could be emptied. Then he emptied a load on her rug. She leapt up in horror. Until he turned it on. Then in a few strokes he was all done and it was all gone. Now he pulled back the cover from the bed. She was in terror that her sheets were unclean. Then he pulled back the sheets, and started vacuuming the bed. "Do you realize what this is?" he asked her. "Do you realize what this is?"

"What this is?"

"It's human sediment."

Now he was asking her how many times a week she vacuumed. She was wondering what to answer. What was the right answer? That she felt humiliated. How she wished she could afford this thing!

Had she realized, he wanted to know, that it came with a very special attachment, one that sharpened knives and polished silver?

Polished silver? They *had* been given a silver tray as a wedding present. She would just bring it out and he could perform his demonstration with it.

And now the demonstration begins. This wasn't supposed to happen! How did these scratches get across the face?

"This wouldn't have happened if it had been real," the salesman informed her.

"Oh dear," Ann said. "This wedding gift is only real on the surface."

His Birds

THE LEAVES WERE TREMBLING. At last the wind died as the evening began to rise. Ann stood by her car with the grocery bags struggling to free themselves. Something huge, then, perched on a post, flew up, and Ann could see by the particular juxtaposition of head and wing and the way he called in the moon also rising the great horned owl.

The call and songs of many birds were starting to appear out of the general music. Ann called back to them: red-winged blackbird, western meadowlark, quail like a bicycle bell, owl, hawk and duck. And they each danced differently in the drafts of swirling sky.

While Ann was preparing dinner Ben pored over all the books he had taken out of the library that day. They were all about birds, with many personal accounts and pictures. This was the beginning of his devotion.

Now, wherever they went, Ben would be able to talk about birds, and he was soon identified with those birds as an expert. Ben stood in the window looking out, hoping to see a great horned owl that night. Ann was also looking out a window. She was seeing herself in the window, doing the dishes.

One day Ben read in one of his books about the call of the great horned owl. The owl, it was now clear, was Ben's totem. He understood it and it understood him. He read how the great horned owl calls to his mate, or to a female, and how she calls to him. Sure enough, Ann had heard that many nights.

And it was true, the book said, as Ben read it to her while she folded laundry, that if a man practices the call himself, that he could call out to the owl, whether male or female, and the owl would call back. It wouldn't know the difference. This was the beginning of Ben's nocturnal wanderings.

It continued, when they went into company, that if ever a question of birds came up all such questions were referred to Ben. And when these people were up on the hill it was Ben they turned to hoping to see birds. But for some reason, whenever in company, either on the hill or down in town, neither Ann nor Ben ever mentioned the evenings Ben stole from the house in the gathering twilight, hooting. Ann never knew for sure whether the owls were calling back. It wasn't really clear.

Then one morning Ann had to leave the house while Ben was still sleeping. She tiptoed to the door holding her breath. She wondered what Ben was going to do here all day alone. Perhaps Mavis would come over and they would catch up on some of the work that was keeping him so late at the office. Ben was too hard on Mavis, Ann thought. She wasn't really such a birdbrain.

Ann was on her way to the city sixty miles away to pick up Ben's little son, Bobby, for the weekend. She released the brake and started rolling down the hill. It was then that she saw it, perched on a pole. She could see its horns and its head moving from side to side. For a split second she was dazzled by this owl in broad daylight. Then she felt terrible that Ben couldn't be there to see it instead of her. After all, they were his birds.

Tossing It Off

WHEN ANN ARRIVED HOME with the groceries she found Ben tossing a coin high in the air. "What would you like for dinner?" she called from the pantry where she was putting the food away. "Tails!" he called. She came into the kitchen in time to see the coin come down, roll across the counter, and land tails up. She had expected to find Ben working on the shit work he had been putting off. But it seems he was having an extraordinary run of luck. His powers were phenomenal, even to him.

Ann started to cook. It seemed that Ben was uninterruptable. Up the coin went over and over and down it came. Strange expressions passed across his face. He was making calculations with a pen on the palm of his hand. This shit work which Ben had told her he would be doing all day was a drag, but it would bring in some extra money which they could use right now. Ann didn't know where the money was going. As she took out the trash she heard Ben ejaculating.

As she set the table she worried that his luck might be turning. The coin continued to rise in the air. But what goes up must come down, roll across the counter, and land the way he called it, he assured her. He wasn't coming in to dinner.

Ann's dinner was getting cold. Apparently, Ben's powers of prediction were quite phenomenal. She wanted him to eat, but she didn't want to break the spell. But finally he came to the table. He ate quickly without seeming to notice that it was his favorite dish. "I'm almost done with this experiment," he said to her accusingly, as if she had been nagging him. Ann had been trying her best not to nag him or to look like she might nag him. His first wife had nagged him. She had not been good enough for him.

This shit work he was supposed to be doing, Ann thought, as she washed the dishes, *was* horribly meaningless and tedious. She didn't blame Ben for not buckling down to it. Perhaps she could help him with it somehow. She sniffed the armpits of his shirts as she gathered the laundry.

"Of course I can help him!" she thought, as she drove back up the hill three hours later with clean laundry and a six-pack of his favorite beer. She hoped he had not done it all without her already as she opened the door with her nose because her hands were full. But as she walked in she heard the familiar click and roll. She set the laundry down and tiptoed into the kitchen. "Oh, there you are!" Ben said. He stared at her accusingly, as if she had accused him of not doing his shit work or wasting time. She looked around the kitchen. Things were not as she had left them. There was a long trough of tin-foil going up and down the entire length of the counter. "Don't you want to know the results of my experiments?" Ben asked, hurt.

"Of course I do!" Ann said, going to hug him.

"I have discovered," Ben said, "in fact, I have proven, to my own satisfaction at least, that although you might have a run of luck, there is no way of actually predicting for sure when it will end." Ann put her arms around Ben and held him tight.

"That actually is a conclusion I came to a few hours ago while you were fooling around down in town. What I've been doing since then is something actually even more amazing. I've found that if I toss the coin in just the right way, that it will roll all the way down one side of the counter and up the other. To this end, I've made this little trough with aluminum foil for the coin to run down. I couldn't get it to sit flat, so I had to use more and more, in fact a whole roll, to get it just right. Better put tin-foil on your shopping list."

Ann looked at the strange trough which went down the whole length of her kitchen counter and back again. She wondered how she was going to be able to continue cooking under these circumstances.

"I still had a little trouble getting it to lie flat—until I thought of nailing it to the counter," Ben said.

"Do you mean you *nailed* it to the counter?" Ann asked.

"Yes, although it took me awhile to find where you put the nails," Ben said. "It was the most reasonable solution to the problem. Why shouldn't I nail it to the counter, anyway?" He looked at her with suspicion.

"Well, I'm going to have to use the counter sometime for cooking," Ann said.

"Well, then we can simply pull the nails out," Ben said.

"But the nails will leave big holes in the formica, and this isn't our house!" Ann said. "What will the landlord say?"

"Oh, Jesus!" Ben said, disgusted. "Why are you making such a big deal over a few little nail holes?"

The Present

IT WAS ANN'S BIRTHDAY, but she didn't expect that she would get a party because she wasn't a little kid anymore. Bobby was a little kid, and he always had birthday parties which were never as much fun as Ann wished they would be. Some little child was always crying, and then there was the unfortunate boomerang, the idea of some manufacturer, and seven stitches. If only they all could have somehow arrived at the beach, but the air was trying to rain, squeezing out tears, and all the soda pop, hot dogs, and paper plates with mustard were in the living room. Not that it ever threatened to rain for Ann's birthday; hers occurred in the hot dry dead part of the fall.

It was Ann's birthday, but she didn't expect that she would get any presents, not because Ben didn't love her, but because birthday presents were an idea of the manufacturer, and Ann deserved a present neither more nor less on this day than any other. Were not all the days of the year the same? Why should some get special treatment over others?

If Ben had displayed his affection in this manner it would have simply been a *display* of affection. It would have been an obligation, a duty, and what had true love to do with these?

Certainly Ann never gave *Ben* a present on his birthday. She tried as best she could never to mention it. She didn't want to remind him that he was growing older, and some day he would die. She herself couldn't bear to contemplate the idea that he would die, that he would die sooner than her, for he was not only older, he was a man.

Ann had made the mistake of giving Ben presents early in their relationship. Until she realized she was buying the commercial idea. Was she trying to make him feel guilty for the fact that he never gave her any presents? No! She wouldn't do that to him. She would stop.

One couldn't expect to be happy on one's birthday. Candles burning and laughter and love with yellow flowers and pink and white sweetness only existed in the imagination without guilt and a ripple of nausea.

Ann didn't regret the fact that she wasn't going to get any presents on this day. She wasn't going to feel sorry for herself. She tried never to feel sorry for herself. She knew that feeling sorry for herself was a flaw in her character. And, what's more, it made her unattractive. So she didn't want any presents. So she was shocked when she saw *two* presents waiting for her on the table.

For a moment, Ann's heart flew to her mouth. But neither was from Ben. Both had come in the mail. One was from Beverly Hills and the other was from Portland, Oregon. Ann ripped away the wrapping.

Although one was small, and for spreading, and the other was long, and for piercing, both Ann's parents and her sister had sent her knives!

Ben laughed. He seemed to think that there was some message attached to this. But actually Ann was glad to have them. These were good, strong knives, she explained to Ben. She needed them. The only ones she had were weak and dull.

"But you'll cut yourself!" Ben protested.
"No I won't," Ann promised. "It's actually easier to hurt yourself when the knife is dull."

The Face

THE HILL BELOW ANN'S WINDOW rolled and undulated without perspective. On it, there was nothing human to be seen, except for one clump of trees the woman who had preceded Ann at this window had used to see as a stagecoach and horses racing across the hill. Racing, and yet standing still. She had pointed it out to Ann one day when she returned to pick up a few of the things left behind from her marriage which were now in Ann's way. Ann hadn't seen the stage yet. She had barely seen the trees. She didn't really want to see a stage, but now there it was, every time she looked out.

That woman who had used to live here was not here now; there was nobody here watching Ann watching out the window, watching the view marching way down to the south where the edges continued without her. Ann sat very still. There was no sound. Then something irrational scraped against the house as if in anguish. But it was only a rose briar which nobody watered.

Ann did not want to bother Ben with it. She herself would do it. She would get up from the window and go through the door into the gusts which filled and depleted the empty landscape. Out there where there was no escape.

Ann sat in the window. No one was here. Motes of dust made a grating, grinding sound. Inside the brain-box the scraping continued.

When Ben returned the next day from his business trip down in town he found Ann glad to see him. But she had a funny way of expressing it. She was curled up in bed not even reading. And he had thought she was going to get some weeding done while he was gone! What had she been doing with her time? Had she regressed, reverted to being a little child? He had been working all weekend down in the town, and he didn't have the energy to play around.

Ann didn't speak. If Ben couldn't see what she wanted, how could she deserve to want it? There *was* work that had to be done in the house. *Somebody* had to stay home. *Somebody* had to go down to the burning town to attend to business. And, if a person is already down in town, why shouldn't that person also visit with friends and stay out all night?

Tears were rolling down Ann's cheeks. She was clenching her breath. She wondered if Ben could hear her from the other room. As she heard his footsteps coming down the hall she turned off the light. She listened to him pulling off his clothes in the dark. Now he was in bed beside her, not far from her. He did not touch her. Then she rolled against him, as if in her sleep. He opened up his arms and tucked her hand against his chest. "I'm really sleepy—" he said.

The next day, however, Ann told Ben that she'd like to go with him to town the next time business called him down. "Is that why you've been sulking ever since I came home?" Ben asked. Ann hung her head. "Is that what you really want to do?" Ben asked. "Why should you possibly want to?" He was sure she would be bored. But she insisted. She wanted to know more about the business.

It seemed that a lot of it took place in bars. And it was true, Ann didn't really like to drink. She looked down into her beer. It seemed like they had been sitting there for a long time. At first, Ann had tried to listen to Ben describing a "deal" to his secretary, Mavis. Now Ann noticed that her mind was wandering. She was listening to the music that was crashing from the jukebox, a song about true love forever. Ann looked at Ben's profile. Any woman would admire it. How could she be so lucky?

Over in the corner some people were playing pool. A big man was playing against a child—a little girl. Ann hadn't known that little girls were allowed to play pool. She would have asked Ben if little girls were allowed to play pool, but he and Mavis seemed to be discussing something important and complicated. Ann didn't want to be the one who made them lose their train of thought.

She yawned. It seemed awfully cold in here to her. And wasn't it awfully late for that little girl to be up? Now she was smoking a cigarette! Didn't she have any respect for herself?

But now the little girl comes around the other side of the table and faces Ann to take aim. Now Ann has to see that the little girl has breasts and hips! She leans her head low now under the lamp until she is exactly behind the 8-ball. How foolish Ann feels as this face comes into focus. This is no child, but a dwarf woman, and her face is marked with terror and woe.

Going to See Ann and Ben

Both Ann and Ben loved it when dear friends came to visit, for they could see through *their* eyes the starry skies and blue blue skies, the wonderful view—even the kitchen table where they always ate pie. Still, before the friends arrived, the house had to be made to make sense. This was not easy to arrange.

Ann had to pray that Ben would go away and leave her a day ahead, at least a day. She never vacuumed in front of him. It made him scream very, very loud in order to be heard. What if he were to walk in suddenly while she was doing it!

Luckily, Ann usually got in her time alone with the vacuum. And she scraped away at the house until she saw how beautiful it was, and how beautiful it was to live here!

"And also," they told their dear friends, "at other times of the year!" Then they all drank another beer.

Ann and Ben loved to have dear friends come to visit and to sit in the same room late into the night and rise at not an early hour to breakfast prepared by guests on the sun deck.

What food they all ate! What jokes they all told! What walks they took together behind the house in the moonlight that must always be shining here.

Ann and Ben, indeed, were renowned in their circle of friends for their hospitality and its happy situation. When one visited them one was on a vacation.

Of course, sometimes even the dearest of friends will stay too long. Ann would not realize this until she realized that Ben had not returned to the living room. Had not returned from the liquor store. Had locked himself in the bedroom. She expects that these guests believe she knows where Ben has gone. The host simply doesn't disappear. "Ben's not feeling well," Ann explains. Though that is not the explanation.

But sometimes friends come without a reservation. Then Ann wipes her hands on her apron. In front of her Ben has been reading the paper. They both have seen the station wagon. Their dearest friends, the Middlemonths, are coming unannounced. Ann glances around the room quickly to see if it makes any sense.

Ben has her in a clench. Her arms are pressed behind her, his hand is cupped over her mouth. There is a knocking at the door. Ann can't remember if it's locked. The Middlemonths are calling their names! Are they going to try to open the door? "Tell them to go away," Ben breathes into her ear. Then he pushes her firmly towards the door.

"Hi!" Ann whispers, when she opens the door as one behind her closes. The Middlemonths embrace her, but she draws away. "I wish I could ask you in," she says, "but . . ." And at this point Ann makes up a pretty little story. That was how Ann got in the position of lying to her friends.

Playing Telephone

A MAN'S HOME is his castle, but most people, Ann and Ben surmised, did not actually respect personal privacy, probably because their private lives weren't worth preserving. These were those typical Americans who ran to answer the phone even if they were screwing.

And they had the concomitant fault of expecting Ann and Ben to leap up from whatever compromising position they might find themselves involved in just because some machine on the kitchen wall was throbbing blindly. But Ann and Ben were not Pavlovian dogs. There was little chance that they would be able to resume lovemaking once the outside world had got them to answer, and wasn't maintaining these positions they had reached the highest good, more important than anything?

If it were really important the person would call them back later. They could always be reached through the mail. If something horrible had happened, they were better off not knowing about it.

A telephone should not dictate how one lives one's life. The telephone should never invade the bedroom, or the study. Anyway, it couldn't; the cord wasn't long enough. Ann and Ben unplugged the phone when they were sleeping, bathing, or sitting in their studies. The telephone was trying to disrupt them. So they restricted it to the kitchen, and there it hung from the wall. Now when the family and whatever guests present were eating any of a number of meals the phone might ring, and those sitting right there at the table a few feet away might not be conscious of that fact, for when it was first installed Ben had taken it apart and opened it up and stuck something between the bells so that they would no longer touch, and then he had taped them down, so that the only sound they now made was a shudder. Still, occasionally this shudder was noticeable above the laughter and conversation.

Then whoever answered the phone and whoever eventually spoke did so in front of everyone seated around the table. Sometimes the people at the table would speak to the person who was simultaneously speaking on the phone. Then that person would have to decide who to listen to—the voice coming from the table or the voice coming out of the receiver. Sometimes there was so much talking and laughing coming from the table and so much thumping coming from the stereo that it was difficult to hear what the voice coming through the receiver was trying to say.

Many times Ann and Ben's friends complained—although to no avail—that Ann and Ben were hard to get hold of. But a man's home is his castle, and Ann and Ben fought to keep it that way. Still, one day, one or two days, as Ann came walking in with the groceries she heard Ben's voice in the kitchen sounding very excited and upset. She heard then the cradle of the phone smash. Ann froze. Everything seemed quiet. However, as she stepped into the room Ben let out a scream.

She had startled him. She should know better than to sneak up on a person.

"Who was that on the phone?" Ann asked, casually.

"What phone?" Ben asked. "Oh, that was nobody important. Just the office. Just some business begging for attention."

"Can't they leave you alone on the weekend?" Ann wanted to know.

"Apparently not," Ben said, but his attention had obviously shifted to other things.

"You should tell your secretary that they have to leave you alone on the weekend. You're working too hard. You need some escape from that place!" Ann said.

Suddenly Ann was covered in juice. Ben had been drinking a glass of juice, and now it was all over her. He had flung it at her. She must have said the wrong thing. She must not have been thinking.

Now he had left the room. She could hear him lying down in the bedroom. She wanted to go in and mollify him, but she was afraid to. She started to wipe the juice from her body and from the wall. Then the phone started to shudder.

"Hello?" Ann said, trying to make her voice sound normal.

"Hi." It was Margery.

"Hi," Ann said. "I can't talk very loud because Ben's trying to sleep."

"Is everything okay?" Margery asked.

"Not exactly," Ann said, in a very low voice.

"Can you talk about it?" Margery asked.

"Not exactly," Ann said, in a very low voice.

The Change in the Weather

ANN AND BEN had moved from the city in the springtime and all summer long Ann reveled in what had been for her heretofore a literary and romantic condition of living close to the earth. She had never actually known before what it was to watch things grow and wither, nor had she been before so aware of the weather. Each morning she saw from the window the weather sucked back, very far back to the sea. Then, as the day rode higher, it would start to move towards her, coming faster and faster all the afternoon, and still, although it happened every afternoon, it was a shock when the weather was upon her.

There were days, of course, when it never arrived; then at night the earth reeled, and above the still warm hillside all the heavens swirled. More often than not, now, the mist hung and dripped from the trees. In it, then, and sometimes at night, Ann and Ben took little walks to just over the rise.

From there they could sneak back up on the house. Then the house would appear suddenly, windows glowing so warmly with a bright golden heavenly light, that it seemed to them, these wanderers, that life inside this hermit's hut, this shepherd's cottage, this lovers' nest, was cozier and more dear than anywhere on earth. And they wondered if the inhabitants would welcome them as wayfarers of the trail who had lost their way, they wondered if the fire would be burning merrily, if there would be steaming cups of cheer in there, and if they would sleep there, deep beneath down comforters, a deep, deep sleep.

And every day that she could, Ann loved to roam far afield and free. And together Ann and Ben climbed the highest hills and probed the deepest valleys. They walked among the cows and sheep, there was no barbed wire fence they couldn't penetrate or creek they couldn't leap. By leaps and bounds they grew familiar with everything that grew, blossomed, and prickled. And then gradually, everything began to slow down, until there was a silver glint in the grasses, and then it started to rain.

At first it seemed like it was just a passing storm. Grey-brown puddles filled the field. The branches of the trees standing all around began to shake and toss, and the trees bent down. Then the rain smeared on the window, obliterating the view. So day and night came back together.

Ann and Ben tracked mud into the house. They had gone to get kindling, but the kindling was wet. They tried to light the fire, kneeling by the cold stone hearth, and the rain poured forth, through the porous stone, and the stone wept. The storm pushed at the big window, and the window buckled, and the rain seeped in. The rain beat at each plank of the house, and through each crack and through each flaw the rain streamed in, and it wept in the room.

Down the Garden Path

In This Bed

The lavender bush never dies. It gets smaller. It is overlooked down here where one seldom passes.

On the other hand, to the left if one looks away from the house, is the camellia which refuses to flower. It is still wearing its original tag, picturing the kind of camellia it is, a very washed out piece of paper.

The azalea beneath it is also dying for no apparent reason, and the rhododendron is only a token of the forest where the tall foxgloves with their purple blossom thrive.

But now the foxglove is tired and would like to take a little nap. It would like to lay its head down in this sweet strawberry patch. But here brambles are waiting to rip it to shreds!

The Tangled Plant

Here a tangled plant lives that doesn't know why it exists; it persists, without hope of ever getting straight. It just assumes that it's wanted.

While it exists, it's almost impossible to see what's becoming stunted or choked beneath it.

But what does it matter? They were only babies, baby leaves with baby blossoms. And now they are no more. That's all. The strangling tangle plant has wiped them into the dirt.

The Listening Tree

This is the tree that's pretending not to listen, but actually *it* started the whole thing. Ann was not entirely aware which tree the branches she was watching waving in her window went to. In her wanderings outside the house when she came up against the trunk of this tree she didn't see its branches. But, it's true, she rarely came up against the trunk of this tree. She came up against the mock orange in front of it. She wouldn't see the huge trunk of this huge tree which was taking over everything, both the garden and the house, while Ann was not aware of them.

Ann Ventures Out

Ben had many projects going at once in the peripheries of the garden in the furthest extremes of the property invisible from the house. There was the gatepost of the future entrance into the potential goat pen to be set into cement. There were the rose bushes to move from one side of the driveway to the other and back again and the holes he would dig for them after he had soaked the ground with his hose. There was the pair of Italian cypresses, the tree that grows in graveyards, side by side and staggered in reference to the setting sun.

Ben had many tomatoes to water, and they needed, he informed Ann, to be watered slowly. He moved the hose patiently back and forth as it dribbled. These plants, overbearing with fruit, needed to be staked. He pounded the stakes deep into the dirt. The dirt needed to be fertilized. He needed shit.

Sometimes Ann wondered if he really *was* out in the garden.

If the phone rang for him she would say, "just a minute," and go to the porch to call his name. There was no answer. She went to call from the back door, but still there was no answer. She started walking down the driveway. She walked up and down and on each slope of the property. But there was nobody. When Ann got back to the house there was nobody there, either.

Ann did not always see the sense in each little project Ben worked at out in the garden, but she always assured him that they were marvelous when he asked her how she liked his fences which fell down as soon as they were erected or his gates which just stood there without fences, shut and bolted fast. Who was Ann to judge? She couldn't picture how everything would eventually come together some time in the future. She stepped over another pile of rotting lumber.

But one day when Ben had been away for several days on business, Ann noticed that the sun *did* shine very brightly in the yard. She went to the garage to get a spade. There was a project out in the garden which wanted *her* attention. She must try to resurrect the bed closest to the house. For while Ben had many projects started at the very end of the garden, the bed closest to the house had gone untended.

Once flowers had grown in this bed, but some years ago there was a terrible frost, and the flowers had blackened and died. Then this bed was brown and bare, and then the rains came down and the thistles began to grow all down the path and up to the house. These Ann had suffered because of their intimidating spikes.

Now she approached them. She was soon surprised at how easy it was, actually, to bring down these foes, for the spiky thistle has neither muscle nor heart, and is easily pulled apart.

The Blockage

ONE DREARY CHRISTMAS DAY little Bobby went to his real mother's for the holiday. There wasn't any holiday here. How could one day make up for the rest? Ann wanted to know. This day was colder and darker than most days, perhaps because little Bobby had left a hole in the house.

Dear friends were about to make their yearly visit. Through the eyes of these houseguests, Ann and Ben would be able to see what a wonderful life they were living. They were no sooner there long enough for everybody to have looked into the toilet when it was Ann's turn. She no sooner left the fire smoking and was alone with herself in the can when she was flush with what she was forced to see. She flushed and flushed, but could not dispose of it. The more she flushed, the worse it got. The swirling mass rose higher and higher. It was running. It was going to overflow.

She returned to the living room, joining her guests. Ann

was afraid. It was a holiday weekend and her plumbing was illegal. Often Ann had wanted to have a baby, but Ben would never hear of it.

Ann moved alternately between the living room where everyone smiled pleasantly and the bathroom where the turds floated around and around. The hydrangea bush under the porch began to reek of urine.

Finally, a plumber agreed to come, although it went against his conscience. He was but two hours alone with the toilet when he presented Ann with the bill. There was nothing he could do. He washed his hands. The toilet emptied into a tiny redwood box on the western slope above which grew a willow tree fed by shit until it got taller and taller and bigger and bigger and its roots got broader and broader and filled the little box all the way up, pushing the shit back up the pipes, killing its only source of pleasure. It would be dead within two years.

Ann needed a snake. Many times, Ann had considered adultery, especially with her neighbors. The snake unwound into the ground. Ann would do anything for the man with the snake, but he presented her with a bill, and told her he could do nothing for her.

The smell of urine was taking over her world. The annunciation had come, actually, two months earlier. Ann had been away from home, on her way to a night class. She was walking from her car to the classroom when suddenly there was a large crash of thunder. Suddenly the wind began to blow at a hundred miles an hour. Then a heavy torrent of rain crashed down upon her, wetting her to the bone. She was in ecstasy.

That night, however, when she came home, she saw that the huge retaining wall next to the house was now leaning over it, and there was nothing to stop the hill that it held back from falling into the house. The pity was, the wall had been a work of art, and the real pity was that the hill felt better without the wall.

But Ann ignored God's warning, and that's how she found herself sitting outside on a chemical toilet, grateful to be sitting here! It had been her father's idea. It would be months and months, months of going outside in the rain to pee. Somehow, Ann preferred it this way. Once she escaped from the house she was free, and sitting with the rain pattering all around her and the door flung open in the dark she was at peace.

The Model Couple

IN THE COMMUNITY where Ann and Ben lived there was one remarkable couple, whom everyone loved, who had been married for about seventy years. They had run away together when they were very young. Their romance would always be in flower. When in company, the company would love to hear the stories they told, over and over, sometimes one telling, sometimes the other, about the events in their long life together. These two were, indeed, an institution, and an inspiration.

What they knew about each other, down to the last detail! How their lives deepened, year after year!

"Or," Ben said, but only to Ann, and only after they had been married for several years, "how they are in prison!"

Ann wanted to see it that way, too, because she wanted Ben to be right so that she could believe in him until the end of time.

Who Else Would Think So?

BEN MADE ANN feel she was special. He loved the little things she would do to make him laugh—little skits and dances. But sometimes, in company, he would ask her to perform. She would have to refuse—all her movements were spontaneous. After all, she was not a trained dog, she was his wife, and only he could appreciate her. He would say what she was like or likely to do or say to a stranger or acquaintance sitting in the bar while she herself was sitting there, and sometimes he would ask her why she was so quiet—until she learned to talk (more than a dog could do), until she could please him, and he said that he understood her and just wanted to help her. He was counting on her understanding. Who else would understand him? What they had was special. He loved the meals she cooked. He thought she was doing a marvelous job—better than he could do. There was no one else like her, and who else would ever think so?

The Wife in a Box

ANN KNEW THAT BEN had been married before, not only to Beth, the real mother of little Bobby, but before that, also, to another woman, Mimi, an artist, whom Ann had never met. Ann liked to hear stories about Mimi, the woman who had loved Ben when he was very young, long before Ann had had the opportunity to know him. And in the stories Ann would fantasize that *she* was Mimi. And Ann loved Mimi, even though she and Ben would never see each other again. That was not, however, how Ann felt about Beth, whom she saw all the time.

Beth, unlike Ann, had chosen to cross into middle age, but Mimi, like Ann, was forever young. (At least like Ann when she had first met Ben, some years ago now.) Beth had just been a seven-year interim relationship between Mimi and herself.

Of course, there were ways in which Ann was unlike Mimi. Mimi used to like to fight. That's why she and Ben, unlike Ann and Ben, had broken up. Ann didn't see the point of fighting.

Beth and Ben had broken up as soon as he had gotten up the courage. But not before she had gotten a little screaming baby out of him. The little baby had screamed him out of the house. Beth had been more in love with the idea of having a baby than she was with Ben. No one was more in love with Ben than Ann.

At least, that was what Ann always assumed.

One ordinary day Ann was home alone. Ben was away on a business trip. She used to resent Ben for not taking her along, but she no longer did. She realized how happy she was to do exactly as she pleased.

She decided she would clean out some cupboards. The cupboards had started out fresh when Ann had first met Ben, but over the years had collected layers of memories, and some of the memories predated even Ann's existence. For instance, take this tin box with the lock on it.

Ann had seen this tin box with a lock on it for years, but had never been shown what was inside of it. For all she knew, there was nothing inside. But it was heavy.

Ann knew that she shouldn't look into the box, look into what Ben did not show her about himself. She was afraid as she tried the lock.

It opened. Ann began to leaf through the papers. Some of them were clippings from Ben's college newspaper—the place where Ben and Mimi had met. And here was a large glossy picture of Mimi. Here was an old menu from a restaurant. More pictures—Mimi in different poses. A lock of hair. Ann hastily shut the lid. But it was too late. Ann had seen it: a wife in a box.

The Terrible Stereo

ANN AND BEN had a terrible stereo. It was very cheap. They had bought it from the previous occupant. It was very large; they didn't know how they could get it out. It was a bargain in the shape of a blond wooden coffin standing on four legs with a lid that opened with a hinge. It played stacks of records indiscriminately, or its radio played loud enough from its corner (horrible to look at) to obliterate not only the birds and the bushes and the incredible silence, but also each member of the house from the other.

Its speakers were very close together, but it cancelled little Bobby's TV in his room upstairs and the living room where Ben was working on his papers and the study where Ann paid the bills. And it neutralized the atmosphere. No matter that it was ugly.

Their Dog

ANN AND BEN had a dog. It was called the family dog, but Ann fed it and took it to the vet and bought its license and walked it and vacuumed up its fur from the floor and the couch where it wasn't supposed to go but would always sneak onto and no one had the will to make it stay down.

Ben had wanted the dog to live outside in the garage, but Ann had invited it in hearing its whimpering. It loved to come in and sit on the couch by the fire and also to roam free all around the neighborhood.

But one day the dog catcher came and scooped the dog up. Ann had to buy him back from the pound where he contracted kennel cough and a handsome vet bill. Ben proposed putting the dog on a chain fastened to a post in the yard. But Ann couldn't tolerate the sight of the dog so chained up, and she felt herself powerless to build a fence the dog couldn't dig under, and that's how the dog took up permanent residence in the house.

Ann would walk him every morning and would try to walk him in the evenings also. But he mainly spent the winters in the artificial heat half asleep.

Ann and Ben looked at him. He seemed to be getting old. His coat was dull and he smelled like a pelt.

They looked at each other. Where had the time gone? And looked away.

A Message in the Night

ONE COZY NIGHT, while Ben was at work and the storm raged all around the house, Ann sat curled by the fire. Her cat was in her lap and her dog was at her feet, asleep. The fire crackled and danced, and she had long since given up reading to gaze into the flames.

Suddenly her dog woke up and trotted to the door wagging his tail. She was surprised. Ben was not expected home for several hours and never returned until several hours after he was expected, but the dog stood wagging at the door.

She got up and opened it. A young man was standing there. She was surprised. She hadn't heard a car drive up, and who would be out walking on a night like this? He was a stranger, her age or a little older, neatly dressed in casual clothes. His expression was mild, and he very politely asked her if he might have some water.

"Sure," Ann said, and invited him in. He stood by the fire while she went to the kitchen to fill a jug for him. She hummed as she ran the tap, and when she brought it to him he thanked her simply and politely, then took his leave.

Ann stood at the door. She could not see after him into the night nor could she hear his car driving away. A feeling of extreme happiness filled her. She couldn't wait to tell Ben about it.

However, when he heard he was horrified. "It could have been a rapist. It could have been the Zodiac killer," he protested. She was never to open the door to anyone she didn't know again.

"I would have known if he had had evil intent," Ann said. "I would have felt it."

But Ben laughed. He thought it quite ridiculous that Ann should have been visited by an angel when he wasn't there.

The Old Couple

PART OF WHAT ATTRACTED ANN to the house in which she and Ben lived was the fact that it had been built by an old couple who had lived in it when they were very old as many years ago as Ann was old. The garden was elaborate the way old gardens are with the bulbs and perennials of a former time. Ann liked to imagine the little old lady in her faded sunbonnet working in the St. Johnswort and the little old man erecting his weather vane over the bird bath. Sometimes Ann fantasized that she was buried under one of the old couple's apple trees.

Ann looked forward to growing old with Ben growing old until they were just like these old people who were just like these old bulbs forever planted in this bed and forever blooming side by side.

But one day, when Ann was out collecting for the heart fund, she fell to talking with another old woman and old man who lived in another little old house just up the hill. Ann had observed these people from afar, but had never before actually spoken with them. They had lived in the neighborhood many years and had seen many people come and go. They had known, in fact, the old couple who had built Ann and Ben's house for their old age.

"You did?" Ann asked. "Oh, what were they like?" The old man chuckled. "We didn't see much of them. But sometimes we would find *him* hiding in our garage."

"Hiding in your garage?" Ann asked.

"That's right," the old man said. "He would ask us not to tell his wife where he was."

Ann's Parents Visit

ANN'S PARENTS were coming to visit her. They wouldn't stay at her house because Ann and Ben had only one bathroom, and Ann wondered if her parents didn't secretly feel disgust at using the same bathroom as Ben. Not that they ever said anything to that effect—they were always cordial. Still, it was understood that there was a mutual dislike on all sides. How could Ann's parents approve of Ben? He was, though they never said so, too old for Ann. He had been married before and so didn't believe, obviously, that marriage was forever. He was often ill, and they disliked the idea of their daughter spending her days nursing a hypochondriac. Still, they never said anything, but Ann resented being pitied. She disliked the fact that her parents would probably judge that Ben drank and smoked to excess, also, so she cleaned all the ashtrays and put as much spit and polish on the house as she was able to without disturbing Ben or provoking him to accuse her of cleaning up for her parents or of choosing them over him. She had chosen him over them, and now she had to prove to everyone that she was correct, that there is some love in the world that is worth any amount of sacrifice.

Still, it made her sad that everyone couldn't love everyone, and actually, she never gave up hoping that this would actually happen. But in the meantime she had to think up an explanation for her parents as to why they couldn't come over from their motel in the morning. It was hard to explain that Ben needed his sleep and wouldn't be up till noon.

However, when Ann's parents arrived at noon after waiting in their motel room all morning, Ben was nowhere to be found. Ann served them coffee and waited for Ben to appear, but he had disappeared. Ann didn't know what to say to her parents, so she excused herself and went looking for him. She found him locked in his study. He had expected that her parents would arrive around two, when he would have breakfasted and showered. Now it was up to her to get rid of them till then.

So Ann proposed to her parents that the three of them go on a little sight-seeing excursion which brought them back several hours later. Ben wasn't at home when they arrived, but returned in time to be taken out to dinner. Ben acted as if there were nothing unusual about this, and none of the rest of them said anything.

Ann's parents hugged her when they left and asked her if she would like to visit them sometime without Ben, but Ann declined. Ben needed her too much. What would he do if she wasn't there? She wondered.

She was relieved when her parents were finally gone. Ben was right. Her parents always made her feel bad.

Life Insurance

WHEN THE OPPORTUNITY had presented itself, Ann had encouraged Ben to take advantage of the offer—not for her own benefit, of course, but for the sake of little Bobby. Ben would be able to get a great deal of life insurance for very little. However, the time for enrollment was limited, and, in fact, today was the very last day. How Ann had forgotten to remind Ben to take care of this important problem she wasn't sure. Now time was running out.

And he couldn't handle it today because the forms had to be turned in at the office, and today was Friday, the day Ann took the car down to the city to pick up little Bobby and do the week's shopping. "Just forget it!" Ben yelled, throwing the policy at her.

"Why don't you let me handle it for you?" Ann offered. "I can stop at your office on my way down to town."

Now she was on her way down. This would give her a little less time to do her errands, but she would make do. However, when she got to personnel things weren't quite so simple as they should have been. For although Ann was Ben's wife, in the end she couldn't sign for him.

Ann looked at her watch. If she drove really fast she could drive back home, get Ben's signature, drive back to personnel, and then go on to town without little Bobby waiting too long.

But there wasn't any time to spare. So it was annoying to find a strange car blocking the driveway when she got there. She had to park on the street. Then huffing and puffing she ran to the house. But the door was locked. This was strange, considering that they never locked the door. Ann rummaged through her purse for the key. Finally she was in and calling through the house, but Ben didn't seem to be anywhere about. Finally she went out on the deck, and there, sitting quite alone, was Mavis, Ben's secretary.

Ann was surprised, but she didn't have time to be, she had to find Ben. Ann started to ask Mavis, explaining to her about the life insurance she was trying to nail down when Ben suddenly appeared behind her. The odd thing was, he was wearing hardly any clothes. Just some old swim trunks she hadn't seen for years, and these were on backwards. But she didn't have time to question, only to get his signature, and his choice of beneficiary, which wasn't Ann, of course, for while many husbands thought it necessary to protect their wives, Ann didn't need any protection.

The Problem of Being Upright

ANN'S PARENTS bought her a small car when she started graduate school because they were afraid that if they bought her a larger car she would end up driving everyone around. Since Ben didn't drive, however, Ann ended up driving Ben and Bobby and Bobby's friend and the dog and the laundry and the groceries and the garbage to the dump.

One of the many places she drove Ben was to his health club in the city which lay across the plain. Ann realized that it was frustrating to Ben to have to rely on her for his transportation, so she made herself as reliable as possible and available whenever he wanted to go. She realized that Ben must feel powerless, and so she didn't mind that he punched her in the arm as they drove across the plain or threw orange juice in her face when they arrived at the health club. How could she blame him when she and her little car symbolized his humiliation?

One Christmas Day, however, when Ann and Ben were at Bobby's mother's showing Bobby how well all his significant others interacted, Ben collapsed on the floor in a spasm. His back had gone out. After that he declined to ride in Ann's little car any more.

He didn't want to have to stoop to get in. Ann was to get rid of the little car and to get a bigger one. In the meantime, Ben's secretary Mavis would be taking him for rides.

Because Ben could no longer stoop he could not go hunting for a car with Ann. Ann would have to do it on her own. She looked at the ads in the paper, unsure how to proceed. She had to choose the car that Ben would choose if he were choosing, and she couldn't spend more than she would receive for the little car once she had figured out how to sell it. Ben did not help her sell the little car. It was her car. But finally she did sell it, and she bought a larger car with the money, and she hoped that Ben would find the passenger seat comfortable.

However, he didn't. So when he had to ride in the car now he rode in the back seat, reading. This made Ann feel very uncomfortable. Some strange distance had arisen between them which Ann could not fathom. She needed to make the passenger seat more upright and she wasn't sure how to go about it.

Ann's Success

ANN'S WORK was the same as Ben's work, and that was one reason why she enjoyed it so much. Or, perhaps, that was why she loved Ben so much. When she had first met him he was already respected in his field and by marrying him she had been able to share in that respect. When she was very young he had begun to teach her everything he knew, and she was an eager student. She so wanted him to be proud of her! There were times when she thought she should give up, but knowing that he believed in her spurred her on.

Meanwhile, Ben's own work wasn't going so well. Ann knew this was just a temporary setback and that he would soon regain his confidence.

But it was unfortunate that just then an offer came to publish some of Ann's latest findings. At first Ann thought that this was a great opportunity for her. Hadn't Ben been always trying for such publication? Wouldn't this make her famous, a success?

Ben laughed scornfully. Was she going to fall for that trap? This wasn't a decent offer, Ben pointed out. She should hold out for a better offer, he said. He dismissed her letter as if it had been an insult.

In shame, Ann threw the offer away. She never sent back a reply. But it was too late. Ann's success had already reared its ugly head. And that night it moved in between Ann and Ben in bed.

A Poor Return

SERVING WAS SOMETHING which took concentration. Sometimes Ann's aim was off or the force she applied was inadequate or heavy-handed. Still, she enjoyed a good game of volleyball with the gang on Sunday mornings. She liked getting into a sweat and she liked these people they played with. They were a hospitable, warm and friendly group, and it was interesting to see each personality rotate through the positions of the game. She liked to see who always set up to whom, who could slice, and who really cared if they won or lost.

Ben was one who really took the game seriously. Ann was playing on his team. The score was very close. It was Ben's turn to serve, and Ann was at the net.

It was a beautiful serve, and no one could touch it. Now the score was even closer. Ann retrieved the ball from out of bounds, and when she was close enough, rolled it back to Ben who poised, and, calling out the score, served again.

No one could touch Ben's serve, and now the score was tied. The ball came back to Ben, and he poised to serve again, but this time the ball came back. Lenny, who was standing next to Ann at the net, sliced it, and again the other team fumbled.

Now as the ball bounced back towards Ben there were shouts of "Meatball! Meatball!" One more point and the game was won.

Ben poised and served. But this time the enemy easily returned the ball and again Lenny, who was quite tall, jumped up to slice it. But Dave, on the other side, lifted the ball, and Philip sliced it back over the net, right in front of Ann. She stooped to lift it, but her aim was no good, and the ball went flying behind her. She didn't know what happened to it, but Ben must have retrieved it, because suddenly she saw him slam the ball with all his force and then it hit her in the belly and the tears sprang from her eyes.

Ben was silent as they drove home shortly thereafter. He must have felt terrible about hitting her with the ball in front of all those people. Now they wouldn't be able to play volleyball anymore. Ann hated herself for being the cause of Ben losing so great a pleasure. Ann knew Ben had a perfect right to be disgusted with her, for whereas she could often serve well enough, she couldn't return the ball with any force.

The Anatomy of Separation

ONE DAY, when they were in the neighborhood, Ann and Ben went to visit Phoebe. Phoebe and Andy were dear old friends and now that Andy had left Phoebe for a younger and blonder woman named Elsa, Ann and Ben wanted to show Phoebe that they were still *her* friends, too, even though they socialized with Andy and Elsa also. Ann realized it was a delicate situation. She realized that she must act as natural as possible so that Phoebe wouldn't think she pitied her or looked down on her for being thrown away like an old shoe. Above all, Ann realized, she and Ben must be careful not to act as if they had come to examine a corpse.

The house looked different than it had when Andy had filled it. It was more open feeling and less cluttered. There was a sense of necessity rather than show to the placement of objects. They had had too many objects in the house, Ann thought. Now the true lines of the house could be seen. It looked a lot cleaner. There weren't piles of papers and beer bottles everywhere anymore.

Phoebe seemed genuinely glad to see them. Her eyes were bright and her cheeks were flush. She had lost a lot of weight. But then, she had needed to. Ann wished that she could lose some weight. Phoebe's conversation was direct and intense in a way that it never had been before. At least, Ann had never noticed it. Andy had always dominated the conversation. Not that Phoebe had ever seemed to mind. She was always busy serving everybody. But today she didn't offer anything to Ann and Ben.

So Ben went down to the corner grocery for some beer. Phoebe put a blues record on the turntable and, laughing in a most infectious way, started to dance, hugging herself to herself. Ann watched her. It was a surprisingly beautiful dance. She wished she could learn it.

The Dark Light

BEN LIKED TO STAY UP LATE at night and far into the morning so that often when the neighbors awoke from an uneasy sleep in the night they would see the house on the hill burning like a candelabra and, when the farmers awoke to milk their cows, they would see, if they glanced up on their way to the cowshed, the lights on the hill just fading with the dawn. For Ben, when he finally went to bed at about three or four, would neglect to turn out the lights, although all was dark in the bedroom which he now entered where Ann had already succumbed to sleep. She had tried to stay awake so that she and Ben could be on the same time scheme, but sleep had overcome her, and she slept deeply in that room with the heavy curtains pulled across the window.

The curtains leaked no light in the morning, for Ben couldn't sleep if there was the slightest bit of light in the room. Nor could he sleep if there were the slightest bit of noise, so Ann, though she woke hours before Ben stirred, lay very still beside him so that she would not wake him by arising herself. She did this because Ben needed his sleep; his sleep was very important, and the alternative was for her to sleep in the other room, and what was the point of that?

What was the point of their marriage if they didn't sleep together? Ann couldn't see the point.

In the morning, when she did finally get up, Ann went around the house turning off each lamp. Somehow, the lamps burning in the daylight made her feel sad. For they burned, but they shed no light.

He Never Heard

FOR SOME REASON, Ann was awake. She didn't know what time it was because she couldn't see the clock. She couldn't see the clock because the room was sunk in darkness. She didn't want to turn on the light because she was afraid it would wake Ben up. Ben's arm was draped over her making it impossible for her to move. If she moved she might awaken him. She was afraid to wake him up. It was very quiet. She listened to his even breathing. Then suddenly, like a wave hitting the house, there came a terrible noise. It was like the yapping of the dogs in hell. Ann lay pinned under Ben's arm, sweating. Then she realized what it was. It was coming from the chicken farm over the hill where the lights burned all night long. It was the sound of a thousand chickens, screaming. Luckily Ben slept on, and he never heard.

The End of the Trip

BEN HAD BEEN AWAY on business for the last three weeks. He had gone east. Ann had always dreamed of visiting the east with Ben. His colleagues' wives often went with them. But Ann was needed at home—and at Ben's office, for she was qualified to take over for him whenever he wasn't there. She was proud to be so qualified and happy that it enabled him to stay away longer than he might otherwise. He had sent Ann one postcard showing a very quaint place he was taking a small side trip to and saying he wished he were home. Or, more accurately, he said he liked their town better. In the early days of their relationship, whenever they were separated, they each had written every day. Now they were more mature.

Of course Ann had missed Ben—dreadfully—but she had been able to get a lot accomplished while he was gone. She had found a welder to fix the car which she never could have done while Ben was home and possibly in need of a ride, she had waxed the floors which he might have wanted to be walking on were he at home, and she had visited a girl friend she somehow never had time to see otherwise. She had enjoyed, also, taking over for Ben at the office, and she wondered why Ben seemed to hate his job so much for it seemed to her both pleasant and easy. Now everything was in order and Ann had still the whole evening to wash and dry her hair and to try on all her clothes to see which outfit made her the most irresistible, for Ben's plane didn't arrive until three in the morning. Always before, their reunions had been the most intensely romantic sessions of abandonment—well, actually, it hadn't been like that the last time, or the time before. Ben had been too tired.

Ann drank cup after cup of coffee to prime her for the long trip down the road of night. She had had the good sense to call the airport and had found that the flight had been delayed and wouldn't arrive until 4:45. It was a two-hour drive, and so, after one a.m., much later than she had thought she would be leaving the house, she finally set out.

It was a long dark road, but she didn't mind. She knew the way. She could drive it in her sleep. No one else was on the road. She was quite alone. She was looking forward to what lay ahead of her, and kept her eyes out for the sign which said "Airport." Then she saw the sign—"Airport exit—two miles," and she watched on her odometer and took the next exit which appeared, though it didn't look familiar. She soon realized that she had turned too soon, but no matter, this was a broad boulevard, though unfamiliar, and she could just proceed down it until she reached the airport road which she was sure was just ahead in this direction. She hoped she would find it soon, because it was very dark and she felt a chill in the light clothes which made her the most irresistible. There seemed to be a park of some sort now surrounding her car and at this point the moon came out from behind a cloud and she saw the gleaming headstones.

A Normal Evening at Home

ANN FELT A CRAMPING in her bowels. Her neck was sore and stiff. It was having difficulty holding her head up. The skin stretched tight against her face. Her jaw was clenched. Her teeth were being ground. She was clenching her fists. Her breathing was becoming shallower and shallower. Now she was holding her breath. She was biting her tongue. It was a normal evening at home.

The Monster

BEN DID NOT ENJOY playing many games with Bobby and his friends, but there was one game which everybody enjoyed and everybody thrilled to play—everybody but Ann. This game was one of their own invention. It would begin with Ben playing quietly at the piano. Suddenly the chords would become darker, then ominous, then menacing. The children would tiptoe up behind him. Ann would hide in her room as the sounds grew louder and more discordant, and then she heard all the keys on the lower register slammed into and then there were screams in the darkened passageway and she heard the children running and slamming through the doors and she knew Ben had turned into a monster. Ann didn't want to play this game—it was too loud—too wild—and she was afraid to see the monster.

The Useless Dishwasher

ONE DAY when little Bobby was twelve and no longer so little, his mother decided to go back to school in another part of the country and it was decided that Bobby should move in with Ann and Ben for the duration. It so happened that Ann had landed a job that year, but Ben was not working, so Bobby would, theoretically, still get plenty of attention. But since Ann was working she suggested that Bobby help out in the house by doing the dishes two nights a week, and since Ben wasn't working, Ben would do the dishes two nights also, so Ann would only have to do them three nights.

Granted, she was still doing them more than anyone, but this was going to be a big improvement for her as she had always done all the dishes in the past, and there had always been many dishes. Ben was very social and always liked to invite people to dinner, and Bobby had at least one friend and usually three visiting and, naturally, eating. Ann was glad. She wanted Bobby to have friends.

That was a lot more important than a few extra dishes for her to do. She realized that it was her own character deficiency that made her unable to tolerate the sight of dirty dishes lying around everywhere and piling up in the sink. She was trying to improve her character. But in the meantime, she would just gather up all the dirty dishes and wash them. However, now that Bobby was moving in, she was, ironically, going to have less work than she used to.

Ben had never done dishes before because each time she had asked him he had said, "Let's just use paper plates. I always used paper plates before I met you." Ann, however, never wanted to use paper plates or paper pots or paper pans or plastic flatware. That was her own character deficiency which she hoped to correct someday. In the meantime, she just washed all the dishes. But now Ben had actually agreed to do some of the dishes. He couldn't very well refuse in front of Bobby. Ann knew when she married him that Ben wasn't perfect, but she had known that someday he would change.

Now when Ben's turn to do the dishes finally came he didn't touch them on the first day. Since he had two days, he figured, he would do them all on the second day. The dirty dishes lying around everywhere and stacking up in the sink so that it was impossible for her to cook bothered Ann, but she knew it was her character deficiency and she bit her tongue.

Finally, late at night at the end of the second day Ben asked Ann to tie an apron around him. He poured the detergent into the sink and the sink filled with bubbles. He started to soap the dishes. As soon as a dish was all soapy, he laid it on the counter. In this way he spread soapy dishes on all the counters, and the bubbles ran over the counters and slid down the walls. Pretty soon there was no free counter space at all.

"What are you doing?" Ann asked, when she could take it no more.

Ben seemed to find this remark to be critical of his dishwashing methods. There was no reason why he should have to take this kind of criticism. If he never did another dish there would be nothing to be critical of. He removed his apron.

Ann did not pursue the issue. What was the point? Ben was incapable of washing dishes. If she washed them she wouldn't have to watch them lying around everywhere greasy and crusted with food.

And that is how things went from then on until one day when Ann got a call from her friend Jane, one day when Ben was away. Jane's neighbor was selling her dishwasher for practically nothing, and Jane wondered if Ann wanted it. "You certainly need one!" Jane said.

Ann had always resisted getting a dishwasher in the past, but suddenly it seemed like a good idea. This one was very cheap, and besides, Ann was earning plenty of money. There was no reason why she shouldn't spend a little of it on herself.

That night Ben called from his hotel. He had gone to visit friends in another part of the country, and, though he no longer had an expense account, he had rented a car and was driving all about. He had recently learned to drive and had never had the opportunity to rent a car before. For some reason, Ann didn't tell him right then about the dishwasher.

Even so, she was surprised at his reaction when he saw the dishwasher. It was, he pointed out, a horrible extravagance. It was a useless object. Ann should take it right back.

To Ben's surprise, however, Ann didn't take it right back. She had already seen the difference it could make in her life. It was too late to turn back.

How He Liked to See the World

DINNER WAS OVER and their napkins lay crumpled on the table. The guests had brought brandy and the room was heavy with smoke.

"Let's go for a walk outside," Ann suggested. "There's a full moon tonight."

They walked in the orchard. They had brought a flashlight, but they didn't need it. They cast long shadows as they went.

"What time is it?" the guests asked. They could look forward to a long drive home.

"It's midnight," Ben said. "But imagine that it's noon. It's high noon, and everyone's walking around in the daylight, only this is how you see the world."

Ann looked at the world. It looked like a photographic negative. The moon was gone, and in its place was an ineffectual sun. Everything was in place but without color. This was not the first time Ben had made this suggestion. Ann shuddered. He enjoyed seeing the world this way.

The Quiet House

ANN DIDN'T TRICK BEN into marrying her by getting pregnant. She got birth control pills. There was no restraint on their sex life. They were married for love and for lust. They didn't need to have children to hold their marriage together the way some couples did. Granted, there was little Bobby, Ben's son by a former marriage. Ann didn't need to have a child of her own because she had Bobby. And yet, she didn't have Bobby. She didn't have to have that sick relationship that often develops between parent and child.

She could love him more freely because he was not her own, and if Ben got mad at him sometimes she could soothe Bobby and then soothe Ben. She was more objective than they. Hers was a privileged position.

But now Bobby was about to leave for the summer and it was going to be just Ann and Ben—just them. Ben had always said that children were hostages to fortune. Ann wasn't exactly sure what he meant by that—except that he didn't want to have any more children—but she agreed with him. They didn't have to live through their children. They would live for themselves. Their marriage would be enough for them.

However, Ann had gotten used to having Bobby around. She was used to cooking special treats for him and playing games with him. She was used to talking with him about what was right and tucking him in bed at night. She was used to his fingerprints on the wall.

Ann and Ben came back from seeing Bobby off at the airport. They didn't talk on the way back. The house was dark and quiet. "I'm going out," Ben said.

The Toy Which Made Noise

IT WAS AN ORDINARY DAY, New Year's Day, only bleaker. Ann and Ben were home alone together. Ann had looked forward to this time when Ben would not be working, when they would spend some time together. But she was surprised at how ugly the world was when she went out walking the dog. Up ahead on the road the horrible neighbor child was playing with his new Christmas toy. Ben hated this child because he suspected that he stole things and wrecked property because his family was so poor he shouldn't have been born. Ann had not thought to hate this child before, but now she saw that he was, indeed, hateful. He was making his new Christmas toy go, right in front of Ann, and it made a buzz as loud as a chain saw.

This was just the kind of noise to jar someone with a hangover, and a person could be expected to have a hangover on New Year's Day. Ann didn't have a hangover, but Ben did, and his delicate nerves had to be protected. The child seemed to be deliberately following Ann up the road with his terrible noise. Yes, Ben was right to hate this child. Of course Ben was right. It was Ann who was wrong. Ann kicked the toy out of her path.

It was what Ben would have done, she was sure. The silence relieved her. She continued to walk in peace now, without looking back.

When Ann got back she tiptoed into the house. She did not want to disturb Ben's delicate nerves.

But Ann's efforts were in vain. A strangely violent angry woman was at the door. She was yelling at Ben. It was something about a child's Christmas present. It was the boy's mother. Ann hid in the back room while Ben screamed at her to get off the porch.

Shortly thereafter Ann explained to Ben what had happened, and suddenly she found he was pushing her to the floor and pummeling her. Ann was surprised. She had thought that she would have at last gained his approval.

For a long time she lay in the dark on the floor crying. Then she washed her face, and taking some money from her wallet, she walked back down the street to the poor child's home. She explained to the woman that she had a migraine headache, though she didn't deserve to hope that the woman would believe her, and offered the woman ten dollars.

But the woman accepted and invited Ann into the dark little house where the family was sitting around the disheveled Christmas tree. And Ann pitied them.

Without Release

THIS IS A SAD HOUSE where things break and never can be fixed. Where things fade and lose their elasticity. Where things pile up and the dust falls coating everything from ceiling to floor with a dull dull film. And the light fades and a white mist surrounds the house. Inside, the house seems empty, but Ann and Ben are there, bare and in bed, and there they thrash without release.

Part 2

The After Wife

Ann Lay Naked

ANN LAY NAKED in the sun. There was nowhere she had to be, no one she had to pick up, nothing she had to prepare for or endure. No one knew where she was or waited for her irritably. That morning she and Ben had put Bobby on a plane to his mother and now Ben himself was gone forever. The sun was warm, warmer than hands, and the wind in the trees sang a story deeper than a human story. Here sky was blue, bluer than she'd ever seen it, happy blue.

Behind her the French doors opened into the empty house, and the breeze came in, and the house breathed deep. Ann had opened every door and window, and the breeze blew through, and blew the greyness through, and the doors banged as the house breathed, and out the doors all the sadness fluttered, and out the doors and windows all the empty sadness blew.

The Voice Stops

ANN SAT ON THE SUNDECK listening to the birds. The voices that had been crying in her head seemed at last to be dead.

These voices had accompanied Ann on every round of her life, day and night, for all these years, ever since she had discovered Ben's first affair. Even after he swore to her that she was unreasonable, that he would never do it again, each time. These voices told Ann that her life was common, that she was nobody special, and, moreover, that since Ben didn't cherish her, she wasn't worthy of being loved. The voices assured Ann that even though Ben had affairs there was still some hope that one day he would be true to her. After all, she had some of Ben's love; he hadn't left her. However, if he did, and by that fact *then* proved that her life was totally useless, then she should get into the car and start driving north, and drive on and on until she was dead.

When Ann discovered Ben's affairs it was always after they were over—over for him, but not for her. She had to listen hour after hour, as she cooked in the kitchen or as she took a shower, to the voice recounting every sordid detail of Ben's fondling of another. And she would always think that if Ben did ever leave her, then she would go to the midwest and become a middle-aged waitress, although she doubted she could get a waitressing job as she had no experience outside the family. The voice never stopped, and it followed her to bed, and in Ben's arms voices assured her that he wished she were another, or even two others. And so the years passed, and each affair Ben swore was the last.

This time, however, Ann was tired. The sun felt warm on her shoulders, and even though she had heretofore assumed that she hated to be alone, she felt peaceful with the empty house safe behind her. Then she heard the crunch of gravel on the driveway. Ben was returning to pick up some of his things.

For some reason, she did not jump up to comb her hair or to prepare some food to woo him with. She sat very still and looked straight ahead. She heard his footsteps coming through the house. Now he was standing behind her.

She turned to look at him, the man she had married forever. Where now was the charm he wielded over her? She saw the charming face—façade—now peeling, melting back. And as she sat in the quiet, still air she saw his mask fall off, and the death's head revealed underneath.

Evening the Score

NOW IT WAS STARTING to get dark, and the ghosts were starting to peep out from behind each table and chair. Ann saw them, hiding in each mirror. Ann was starting to panic. Ben was gone forever, and she didn't think she would be able to sleep in this house anymore. She didn't know which way to turn. Then she thought of Mark.

For many years, Ann's neighbor Mark had had a crush on her. His ex-girlfriend Lana had told Ann how Mark always trembled whenever she had visited them and Ann had just shrugged her shoulders. And she had pretended not to know how Mark felt about her when he was visiting at her house, sitting across the table with words all choked in his throat.

Ben liked to make fun of Mark because of his brute strength, and so Ann was extra-careful in her relationship to Mark to avoid making Ben even more jealous.

However, on several different occasions when Ann was feeling forlorn because of what she couldn't help but think of as Ben's betrayal, Ann had considered dropping in on Mark and letting him have his way with her at last. In this way, she reasoned, she would be able to stop hating Ben a little bit and could love him more. It wasn't that she wanted to even the score.

However, as luck would have it, Ann never got her opportunity. It was just as well. She didn't really want to face the complication of a double life. Still, it comforted her to have it up her sleeve. And now it comforted her to think that even if Ben had tossed her out like an old shoe there was still one place where she would be appreciated.

Mark's voice sounded sleepy when he answered the phone, but he assured her he was not sleepy; he was in the hot tub. He would be more than happy to let her stay in his spare room, he said. "I'll be right over," Ann said, relieved.

When Ann got there she found that Mark was not alone. A woman, whom Mark introduced as Janie, was already in the tub. But she got out to go in the house to get Ann a gin and tonic.

Ann started to get into the hot water. She didn't ordinarily drink, but found she was soon clicking glasses with Mark and Janie through the steam. After all, she reasoned, she did not ordinarily do anything anymore. Janie was extremely pleasant, and when she was in the kitchen mixing more drinks Ann asked Mark who she was. Was she Mark's girlfriend?

"Oh, no," Mark said. "She's just taking her vacation here."

"Oh," Ann said, not knowing what that meant, but swallowing it.

When Ann woke in the morning she found she was in a very pleasant room. There was a large basket filled with rose petals on the table and some very interesting books—especially one about birth control—on the shelf. That afternoon she went back to her house and loaded up her car with her most precious things. She would stay in Mark's spare room until she figured out a way to deal with the ghosts in her own empty house.

"Where's Janie?" Ann asked Mark when he returned that evening. "She went back to her own house," he explained.

Soon it was time for bed. Ann said goodnight and thanked Mark for letting her stay there. She was grateful that he wasn't putting any pressure on her. Then she went to her room with the rose petals on the table and all her most precious things spread about her and she got into bed and started to read the book about birth control.

For years Ann had used the pill but had given it up a few years ago because she was afraid of dying. She wondered if this was why Ben had wandered. He didn't like the spermicide she had to use with the diaphragm and he didn't want to use a condom. It took all the pleasure out of it for him, so he took his pleasure elsewhere. Nonetheless, Ann still refused to return to the pill. The pill had made her feel drugged and it had taken her body from her. This stubborn rebellion of Ann's was perhaps the first indicator that their marriage was over. Ann was beginning to realize just how complicit she herself was in the break-up. No wonder she felt no urge for revenge on either Ben or his new girlfriend. She had only a literary appreciation of such emotions.

This book, which was Janie's, explained how a woman could determine when she was ovulating and know for sure when she was fertile and when it was impossible for her to conceive. Ann realized as she read that she herself was now in a "safe" period of her monthly cycle. If she were to make love tonight everything would be all right. Ann closed the book and turned out the light.

Now it wasn't long after that that the door of her room opened a crack, and then wider. Then Mark was in bed beside her.

The next day, Ann returned to her own house, but the ghosts were still there. So she just collected a few more things to take down to Mark's, fed the dog and watered the plants. Then she went back down the hill.

The first thing she noticed when she entered the spare room was that someone had spilled rose petals all over the bed and the bed, which she had carefully made, was in a shambles. Then she saw all her own things strewn about as if they had been ransacked and thrown about the room.

Ann was dumbfounded and went to find Mark. She found him out in the yard trying to extricate his glasses from a giant cactus. There were unraveled recording tapes all around him in the grass. "What happened?" Ann asked.

"Janie came back," Mark said.

Ann was surprised. Then she put two and two together. Of course, Mark was more than a friend to Janie. Ann wondered at the difference between herself and Janie. Ann had never beat Ben up when he had cheated on her. She had never ransacked *his* girl friends' things. Ann had been unable to achieve this catharsis. Until now.

One Hundred Eighty Degrees

ANN WANTED TO RID her house of ghosts, but she didn't know how to begin. So she went to see her friend Emily, and Emily said, "What's your problem?" And Ann said, "I don't think I can stay alone in my house because it's full of ghosts." And Emily said, "Pish!" It's a beautiful house and it's your house. You belong there." "That's all very well, but the house is full of ghosts," Ann said. "I wonder if you could tell me how to get rid of them." "Yes, I can," Emily said. "It's very simple. All you have to do is turn everything one hundred and eighty degrees." "One hundred and eighty degrees?" Ann asked. "Yes, you must turn everything around," Emily said. "All these years you've been living in your house you've thought things were going the only direction they could go."

"Yes," Ann said. "I didn't think there was anything better."

"Well don't you see everything's been facing the wrong direction?"

"Yes," Ann said. "You're right." Then she went home and started pushing the furniture around. She pushed the couch back from the center of the room and the room opened up. She pushed the bed against the wall and the bed was now safe. She pushed the table one hundred and eighty degrees and now, when she sat there, instead of looking at the stove and the sink and the counter, she found she was looking at the tops of trees and the peaks of distant mountains and the bright blue dome of the sky.

Ann Sleeps

IT WAS TIME FOR BED. It was much earlier than Ann had gone to bed before Ben had left, but she saw to her surprise that it was more natural for her to go to bed early. She was alone in the house. She could have gone down to her neighbor Bob's and slept on his couch, but to her surprise she found it was nice to be alone. She liked Bob well enough, but she didn't want to have to talk to him. She went to the door and let the cat out,but she didn't lock the door. To her surprise, she realized she felt safer with the doors unlocked and the windows open. Ben had always locked and double locked every door and window and he had a sawed-off shotgun in the closet although there was no crime in the town.

Ann then went around the house turning out the lights. Ben always left lamps on, but to Ann the dark was beautiful, deep and safe.

Then Ann lay safe in her bed on the hill, her heart open in the dark.

The Mystery of the Cookbooks

ANN HAD A MONEY PROBLEM. Her job had ended just when Ben had left, and he had left her with nothing. He had had a good salary, but had somehow spent it all on rent-a-cars and motel rooms. Bill collectors kept calling for him, but Ann didn't tell them where he was. She didn't know. She didn't want to know. Still, she had to raise money. So she decided to sell things. Ben had gleaned what he wanted from the house already; now it was up to her to dispose of the rest. She began sorting through the cupboards she had never dared open during Ben's reign. True, she used to peek into the cupboards when Ben was away, but she had always been careful just to peek and not to disturb the contents lest he suspect what she had been up to. Now she opened one cupboard and a horrible pile of dead shoes fell out. She was not surprised that Ben hadn't taken these. In the next was a pile of rejected jackets and sweaters with holes. Another was completely full of staplers. Apparently, whenever a stapler had run out of staples Ben had taken another home from the office. In another was a shoe box containing a bottle of beard dye and a black toothbrush, in another an envelope full of letters written by a suffering female. Others contained items of like interest. There was not much here that Ann would be able to sell.

Ann stood in the bedroom facing the large oak mirror. She liked the face she saw. It was a good face, a determined face, a face not without grace. How many times had she looked in this mirror and found another face? A sad, tired face? A brittle face? She had looked and looked into this mirror hoping to see the happy face that she wished to see there, and the old oak mirror had looked back, disgusted. It had seen, after all, what went on in that room when Ann wasn't there. It had tried to show her, but Ann wouldn't see. Then one day it had toppled over and hit Ann on the head. It was very painful, but Ann chose to ignore it. But now she saw it. She quickly took it from the wall. She would sell it.

And she would sell all the other mirrors. Why had she and Ben so many mirrors? It was embarrassing. Apparently, she had been accustomed to simply lowering her eyes and avoiding herself.

Here was the gold gilt mirror that Ann hated the most. How many times had it watched Ben primping before leaving for his "health club"? Ann ripped it from the wall. She would sell it. She would sell them all.

Ann went into the kitchen. Surely there were many things here which would fetch a pretty price. Perhaps she could sell some of these cookbooks. After all, she no longer needed them. When she had met Ben she had not owned one cookbook. His last wife, Beth, had given them her old copy of *The Joy of Cooking* when she got a new one. Beth had prided herself on her cooking. Ann had prided herself on other things. Now, suddenly, Ann looked at her cookbooks. There were three shelves of them! She knocked them down. She would sell them. She didn't know how they had gotten there.

Ann Chooses Happiness

ONCE UPON A TIME there was a woman who wanted everything in the world but her own happiness. For many years she worked at perfecting her skills as a cook, housekeeper, career woman, chauffeur, laundress, lover, generous open heart, stepmother, and comedienne, and she had made many people laugh and many people happy, but her own happiness was sorely neglected and finally just sore.

Then one day she died and went down to hell. She was surprised to find how wonderful death was, contrary to what she had always supposed. Indeed, death was a lot better than this life she had been leading where everyone was false and she had to forgive them and the walls were painted bright orange and stripes disguised the door. She was surprised that she hadn't found this door a long time ago, this door which she had fallen out of, for there was nothing, after all, on the other side, and she fell through the air as if she were flying but landed on her feet.

Now there was nowhere else to fall, and she could only go up, up towards heaven with arms extended. And her own happiness, which she had never before thought herself worthy of, and which she had been afraid of all these years, was extended to her, and this time she took it and wore it like a crown.

The Overthrow of the Alphabet

NOW THAT ANN WAS FREE it bothered her to see anything which was not. So she opened the door, and the dog, who had been under constant surveillance these many years, stepped out. He paused on the porch, sniffing the air. Then his coat fluffed out, his ears perked up, his eyes brightened, and he smiled. Ann sighed. There was still an uneasy feeling in the house. Then Ann realized it was coming from the house plants. They were crawling with spider mites and their leaves were brown and curling. They were gazing longingly out the windows where the leaves of the plants who lived in the ground tossed in the happy wind that blew wherever it pleased. "These plants must go free," Ann said, and she carried them all out to the porch. "Sink or swim," she said to them as she turned her back on them and went back inside. Now things were feeling better. However, all the records were out in a jumble and all the books were off the shelves. Ann had never understood Ben's system of categorizing the books, so she put the books back according to size rather than content. From here on in she would have to scan all her books before finding one she was looking for and would therefore become more familiar with her library.

Now she had to attend to the records. She knew these had been organized according to the alphabet, but she was not going to be dictated to or given orders by anyone anymore, least of all the alphabet. She was through with the alphabet. She put the records back in a random order so that it would always hereafter be too much trouble to find one particular record and she would never have to hear the old music of her life again.

What Would Her Mother Think?

ANN FELT LIGHT. Partially because she had stopped eating. She had stopped eating because she had stopped cooking. She had stopped cooking because Ben and Bobby were no longer there. She had no interest in cooking just for herself. It took too much time. She no longer had time to cook five meals a day. Life was not long enough. Life was not long enough to spend shopping. Ann had stopped shopping. There was nothing she wanted. She could exist on what was already in the cupboard. There were cans of sardines and a jar of peanut butter. She kept the jar of peanut butter in her room. Then if she needed to eat she simply had a spoonful. Life was simpler this way. She didn't see why she should spend another minute washing dishes. Ann felt light. She felt like a tremendous weight had been lifted from her shoulders. For years Ann had wanted to lose just five pounds. It had seemed impossible. But now it was gone. Whatever she had to suffer would be easier now. She could handle anything now that she was in control of her body. But that night she dreamed that her mother was angry at her for losing weight. That was strange because her mother would be delighted to know that she had lost weight. But she hadn't told her mother. She hadn't told her mother about the separation.

Their Position

MARGE AND HENRY MIDDLEMONTH were shocked when they heard the news. They didn't understand how this could happen. Ann and Ben seemed to have had the perfect marriage. They had been together so long—as long as Marge and Henry—no, longer. Perhaps there had been some mistake. They didn't want to take sides. They loved both Ann and Ben very much and didn't want to take sides. They just wondered if Ann was all right. Was Ann completely devastated, bereaved? They could understand that Ann was probably totally shaken and they wanted her to know that they were behind her—and behind Ben. And she could count on them. They could only hope for a reconciliation. Anything would be better than this separation. Ann and Ben had been together longer than anybody. Now the Middlemonths would occupy that position. They were very upset and wondered if there were anything they could do.

The Spider and the Fly

ANN HAD DROPPED IN to visit her neighbor Bob, but Bob was not alone. His friend Carl was there. It soon became obvious to Ann that Carl was coming on to her. He tried first to catch her attention. He wanted her to know that he wasn't just a common jerk. He wanted her to know that he was an admirer of grace and beauty. That was why he loved tarantulas. Because of their beauty. He insisted. He really did love them. Carl was large with hairy hands. Ann got up and said good-by. She had to fly. She liked Carl and tarantulas about equally.

Only When He Talked

BEAMS OF PURE GOLDEN SUNLIGHT descended through the trees. The river sparkled, and rushing along over large and larger stones, sang a deep and happy song. Ann was looking up, following the soaring birds and her own heart, loosened from its cruel cage.

Then she turned to look at Billy. Billy had brought her on this camping trip. He had asked her to come after only one night with her. She had been enchanted. Ben had never wanted to go camping because he was afraid of being uncomfortable. But Billy made Ann very comfortable. He did all the driving, planning, organizing and cooking. All Ann had to do was lie back and eat. She didn't know quite what to say, so she just ate and was quiet.

It was easy to be quiet driving along in Billy's van, for the motor was very loud and a large hump separated them. So Ann munched on Billy's homemade trailmix and watched blankly as all the beauties of the earth unfolded before her. This landscape was made for lovers.

And they were lovers, each night going through the motions so realistically that Ann could almost believe that they loved each other.

Billy was both competent and nurturing in a way which Ben had never been. Ann worshipped these qualities in him. It was only when he talked to her that she wondered what she was doing there.

Free Advice

ANN WAS WORRIED that Ben would try to make her move out of the house. She wondered if he owed her anything for support. She wondered what her rights were. She needed a lawyer.

But she was afraid to get a lawyer. She had heard how expensive they were. She was hoping that soon she would get another job, but right now she had less than nothing. She was robbing Peter to pay Paul. Then she remembered that she had had a student in a night school class who was a lawyer. He had not been very bright, and she had gone beyond the call of duty to help him. Now, maybe, he would do the same for her. She gave him a call, and he, sounding very sympathetic, invited her to stop in at his office.

Now he was staring at her across the desk, just as she had stared at him across her desk when he had been her student. He listened to her story—how Ben had cheated on her and beaten her—all she had put up with for all those years—her relief to be free, her intention to rent out part of the house, and her worry that Ben could force her to move. She asked him exactly what her rights were.

The lawyer leaned back and chewed his pencil. Then, taking off his glasses, he told her what, in his expert opinion, he thought she should do. Ann was thinking that if he sent her a bill for this consultation that she would pay, she would have to find a way to pay. "I think," the lawyer said, "that you should try to reconcile with your husband. Boys will be boys."

"Thank you," Ann said, rising. Then she walked down to where she had parked her car, tears of rage welling up in her eyes. A meter maid was just giving her a ticket.

Ann's Sneer

ANN WAS STAYING at George's house when John heard she was in town. He called up and asked if he could come over and see her. He hadn't seen her since she and Ben had broken up. His voice sounded funny. He didn't know what tone to assume, obviously. "Come right over," Ann said warmly.

"That was John," Ann said. "He's coming right over. I remember when his wife left him. He was devastated. Then his guru told him it would take a whole year to recover." Ann laughed. "You see, he was very much broken up when his wife left him and I'm sure he expects to find me equally devastated. He can't imagine how this could be the best thing that ever happened to me. You watch, the first thing he'll say to me will be 'It'll take a year'!" Ann sneered.

In a few minutes minutes John was at the door. He went right for Ann and gave her a big hug. "It's great to see you," Ann said.

"I know how you must be feeling," John said. "You just have to give yourself a year to recover."

Ann looked over at George to give him a wink. But she couldn't. There were tears in her eyes.

What Never Happened

"I REALLY LOVE MY WIFE," George said. "And she loves me. I'll be joining her in Minnesota in two weeks. Maybe I'll go in one week. I'll just call her and see how she feels about that. A good marriage is just the most wonderful thing in the world. Gee I hope you and Ben can reconcile. I know he's been a skunk. I know how you feel. Maggie had a few affairs, too. But it was my fault. I told her she could, but then when she did I couldn't take it. I thought I could take it, but I couldn't. Whose fault was that? Gee I miss her. I wonder what she's doing right now. My problem is that I'm just so angry. I mean, I'm not angry anymore, but I was so angry when I found out about her last affair that I wanted to die. No, I never cheated on her—I wanted it to end right there. I was just so angry, but I didn't want to give her something to get even with. Now she's promised me—we promised each other—always to be true, forever and ever. So she must never know what just happened. So promise me you'll never tell anyone."

"I'll never tell anyone," Ann said.

"And let us pretend between us that it never happened and never mention it."

"It never happened," Ann said, getting out of bed.

"I think I'll go a week early," George said. "I miss her so much. Maybe I won't even write. Maybe I'll just surprise her."

The Explanation

"WHAT I CAN'T UNDERSTAND," Ann said to her friend Emily, "is why I put up with it for so long! Didn't I see how I was being treated? I must have felt that I didn't deserve to be treated any better. But why? Why did I think so little of myself?"

"That's what we all always wondered about you," Emily said.

"I just can't understand it," Ann said. "How could I think so little of myself? What was I so afraid of? Of being alone? It's a relief to be alone."

"You must have gotten something out of it," Emily said.

"Was it just pride?" Ann asked. "Couldn't I ever admit I had made a mistake?"

"You must have liked it," Emily said.

Ann Has Enough

ANN RENTED OUT the upstairs of her house to a nice fellow she would never go for. She had nothing in common with him; she had no interest at all in either astronomy or physics. She hardly looked at him when she spoke to him, and only spoke to him about household matters.

The first thing he did was offer to do her laundry. No one had ever done her laundry before, except her mother long ago. She herself hated doing laundry and always put it off. So she agreed—she would let him do her laundry though she felt a little odd about having a strange man wash her underpants.

The second thing he did was offer to cook her dinner. No one had ever cooked for her before, and though she really didn't want to eat the large meals he cheerily prepared for her, she started tasting them and was soon at the point where it was hard for her to stop.

Then he led her upstairs, and the relief she felt at being held in a man's arms was so astonishing to her that she wondered if perhaps she were falling in love, and immediately started studying astronomy and physics and going out to bars and playing pool and doing all sorts of things she never imagined she would have any interest in doing. But the stars faded and the sun came up and Ann realized she had that bloated feeling that comes from eating too much, and finally she came in to where Erik was sitting by the fire and she told him that there was something she had to tell him. "I don't want to eat with you anymore," she said.

Ann Returns to the Sea

OVER AND OVER and over, and again, and slightly different, slightly different and again, sea green, grey ocean, over and over and over again Ann walked alone down the beach which was always the same, eternal, unchanging, and always different, never the same wave, never the same flotsam, tracks here going on forever and then washed away while the music played over and over and over a roar, and the white spume blew before her like her life.

Ann's Song

ANN HAD THREE JOBS. She had been worried that she wouldn't have even one job; she was surprised at how easy it was for her to support herself. Soon she would be able to pay back Peter whom she had been robbing to pay Paul. Soon she would be able to buy herself a reasonable stereo. Soon she would have the motor of her car rebuilt. For she had to commute.

Ann was tired. She was tired and sick. She had three colds. It was raining and it was cold. But she was proud. She was proud of how well she was doing at each of her jobs. She began to sing. Even though it was raining and she was driving. Even though it was night and she had to work in the morning and her nose was running.

The wind blew against the car and blew the clouds against the moon. But the moon shone and the clouds rushed away. And Ann sang as the moon lit her way.

The Narcissus Bloom

THE RAIN FELL EVERY DAY, on the roof, and on the path, and in the garden the bulbs were reawakened and the narcissus began to bloom. Ann picked bunches, and they filled the house with their sweet perfume. And she picked pink camellias between the storms, and the storms came again, swelling each pond and stream, and the grass began to grow, higher and higher, and it surrounded the house.

Inside, now, Ann removed her boots and her raincoat and went to the kitchen to make herself a pot of tea. This she carried back with her into the bedroom where she propped up the pillows and, snuggling down under an afghan, she began to read. It was a book about a Queen who had many suitors. One loved her, but she rejected him because she knew he didn't really love her, he loved her castle. Another loved her, but she rejected him because she knew he didn't really love her so much as he hated the dead king. Another loved her, but she rejected him because she knew what he really loved was her prestige. So you see, the Queen was quite alone. It was whispered in the kingdom that she mourned the dead king, but this wasn't really true, for the king had been a very evil man. Sometimes the Queen, nonetheless, was very sad, for although she had many suitors, she was sure that nobody loved her. Still, she consoled herself in her loneliness with the fact that at least she wasn't with the evil king anymore or with any of the false princes, especially the one who only loved her for her feet.

For these were very dainty, and she tucked them under her now, closeted in her chamber which was always filled with flowers and content to pass the hours alone in quiet contemplation, sipping tea and listening to the rain.

Their Shame

NOW IT WAS A PLEASURE for Ann to fly down to L. A. to visit her parents. She could give them her full attention and not worry that she was choosing them over someone else or someone else over them. She could accept them lovingly instead of looking at them critically. She could honor them and enjoy them in a way she had been unable to do since she was a child. Perhaps it was because she was no longer hiding anything from them as she had tried to hide Ben's intolerance and her general unhappiness. Moreover, she felt that perhaps for the first time in her life her parents were proud of her, for one of the jobs she had landed was quite prestigious.

"Tell me about your job," her aunt asked her. So Ann started to tell her. She had used to be very close with her aunt.

"And how is Ben?" her aunt asked. "What's he doing while you're down here?"

Ann was shocked. "I don't know," she said. "Ben and I have separated. Didn't Mother and Dad tell you?"

"No," her aunt said. Apparently, her parents hadn't told anyone about her separation.

The Stupid Bedclothes

ANN WAS THROUGH WITH LOVE. She didn't need to prove to herself and the world that she was sexually attractive. She didn't need to prove to strange men that she was good in bed. She didn't need to worry about being pregnant anymore. She didn't believe in throwing caution to the wind and living a spontaneous, carefree life.

"When, when, when will I find someone to love?" the radio moaned. Ann turned it off. Then she got into the shower with her bottle of "Quell."

Apparently, she had scabbies. She had wondered why her wrist was itching so badly. Now she had to wash all her clothes and sheets and bedclothes and apply a hot iron to the mattress. Bad mattress! Naughty sheets! Stupid bedclothes.

How She Felt About Him

OCCASIONALLY, though she tried to avoid it. Ann would hear news of Ben. One day, a mutual friend happened to mention that Ben was doing well—prospering. He was making good money, he and his new girl friend were getting along well, and he was in good health. "Good!" Ann said. "I'm glad to hear that!" But she cursed her friend under her breath for remaining friends with him and she found that she was wishing that his girl friend would leave him and take all his money.

Then one day several months later Ann heard another report of Ben: his girl friend had left him and he had become acutely paranoid. He thought she was involved with a conspiracy to take all his money. Moreover, many friends reported, he looked dangerously thin. Surprisingly enough, Ann felt worse now than when she had heard the first report. "At least some people are still sticking by him," she thought, and she blessed them for still being his friends. Then she prayed that his girl friend would return to him and that he would awaken from his paranoia and once again regain rosy health.

And that is exactly what happened. You can imagine how she felt.

The Conclusion of the Year

NOW EXACTLY A YEAR had passed since Ann and Ben had separated. She had seen the summer blaze hot and blue, she had seen everything die in the fall and she had watched the winter rains washing everything away. Now spring was here.

A year ago she had wondered if she was going to be able to support herself. Since then she had had three jobs. She wondered why she had worried. She wondered why she had considered abandoning her house. Now she was living in her house the way it deserved to be lived in. The way she had always wanted to live in it.

A year ago she had worried that she wouldn't have any friends. But her friends hadn't deserted her. She had many friends. Good friends. They had helped her.

True, her body had gone into shock. It had mourned and it had been afraid. It had become very sick. But now it was better. Now that the sun was shining again. Now that Ann could go swimming every day while the purple wisteria bloomed and the clouds swam in the sky.

She had had a few relationships, also. She had seen the many virtues that different men could possess. She appreciated these virtues. There was also, however, something strange about each. And finally they all remained strangers to her.

Well, wasn't it all right to be alone? She liked to be alone. She sat on her hill watching the branches of the bushes swaying in the breeze. She watched the birds balanced in the trees. She watched the mountains, deep purple in the gathering twilight. The world was beautiful, more beautiful than she had ever imagined. Wasn't that enough?

Part 3

The Marriage Made In Heaven

A Wedding in the City

ANN WAS AT A WEDDING in the city. She hadn't been invited, for, although she was acquainted with most of the guests, she hardly knew the bride and groom. She was crashing the party. She had, however, brought along a present. She hadn't wanted to come to this party, but her friends, Marge and Henry, with whom she was staying down here in the city, had insisted. They had forgotten that they were going to this party when they had invited Ann to come and stay with them. Ann hadn't wanted to come, but finally, after a lot of coaxing, they had convinced her. Now here she was, dressed in her flowered skirt with its ruffle up the side and her antique lace blouse with its open neck.

The room was fairly packed with people, and she went to stand next to Henry. He was speaking to someone she had never seen before, but he looked very pleasant. He smiled at her warmly. Henry introduced them. His name was Abraham.

The funny thing was, Ann was supposed to have met Abraham several months before. They had been invited to the same dinner party, but that had been in the winter when she had had three jobs and three colds. She had not been able to go.

Abraham remembered her name very well, for everyone had talked about her. But now Ann remembered that her friend had gone to the party and that he had mentioned Abraham to her and how much he had enjoyed meeting him.

Henry Middlemonth had melted away into the crowd, but Ann didn't mind. She didn't notice. She was staring into Abraham's eyes as he spoke to her. People occasionally tried to butt in on their conversation, the way people do at parties, talking to one person and looking over their shoulder to see someone else, then talking to that person and looking over their shoulders. But no one could interrupt Ann and Abraham. They did not look over each other's shoulders. They looked at each other's heart.

Finally, after many hours, Henry came up to her and said that they were leaving now. Marge was waiting in the car.

Abraham looked distressed. "Please," he said. "Give me your address." Ann quickly scribbled it on a piece of paper. Then she handed it to him. He looked at her earnestly. She floated out behind Henry to the car. Everything made perfect sense. She had fallen in love.

Good News

ANN WAS CALM. She knew that she loved Abraham though she had seen him only once. She knew that he was in love with her, also, though no word was spoken. Though they had never touched each other. She knew that she trusted him to his last pore, to the end of time, and yet, wasn't that, in actuality, ridiculous? She didn't know enough about him to trust him. This must be a delusion. She knew it must be a delusion, and that is what she told herself. But she didn't believe it. Just then, Erik, her roommate, walked into the house. He was in the process of moving out. He handed her her mail. There was a letter from Abraham. Ann began to read it. It ws a beautiful, warm, funny letter. It was a dear letter. It was a letter written by a good man, a kind man, a deep man, a wise man. At the bottom of the letter was the man's phone number. He asked her to phone him.

"Good news?" Erik asked. Ann was jumping up and down.

His Voice

ANN WAS SAVORING Abraham's please to her to phone him. Just then the phone rang. He hadn't been able to wait. He wondered if he could visit her. On the following Tuesday?

Now Ann savored the days before Abraham came to her. She knew that her life would change its course utterly once he arrived. She was not sorry to see the old life go. She felt peaceful. Once more she walked alone down the beach, but already it was starting to fade, to pale.

When she returned home, her new roommate, Bruce, told her that she had had a phone call. It was Abraham. He had phoned twice.

"Mr. Right," Ann said. Then she took the phone into her room and dialed his number. There was his voice—warm, deep, and friendly. She sat down on the bed. She was beginning to get to know him. She took off her shoes. They were telling each other who they were. His words curled through the wires and moved in her ear. Ann lay back, and Abraham's voice poured over her.

The Bonus

ANN WONDERED how this could be happening to her. It was too good to be true. But it was true. So perhaps it wasn't good. But everything she knew about Abraham was good. Perhaps there was something she didn't know about him that wasn't good. She didn't really believe that that was so, but she decided to call her friend Emily to ask about him. Apparently, Emily knew him. Why hadn't she met him before, she wondered, though she knew why. She hadn't been ready.

Emily sounded interested to hear that Abraham was coming to see Ann.

"What do you think of him?" Ann asked. "Is he trustworthy? Sincere?"

"Absolutely!" Emily said. "And he's extremely good looking!"

Ann realized, with a little surprise, that it was true. Abraham *was* very good looking she saw, now that she thought about it. His outside matched his inside. It was like a bonus.

The Heat Wave

TUESDAY DAWNED HOT AND BRIGHT. Ann went swimming, but that didn't cool her off. The sun blazed hotter and hotter, and the sky was a bright blue. It looked new, like the roses which had just that day decided to bloom. Ann put on her red sundress and went out to pick strawberries. She had told Abraham to come at two, and it was almost two now. He would probably be late, as most people were, and she was too excited to sit still in the house. But she had just started picking when she saw him driving up the driveway. It was exactly two o'clock. She could see his face framed inside the windshield. His head was bowed, but his eyes were raised. Ann realized that this was the face she would love forever.

She went to meet him on the driveway, and as he moved towards her, she moved towards him to kiss him. Then suddenly she remembered that she hardly knew him, and she pulled herself back. She hoped he hadn't noticed. She didn't want him to think her too forward. She invited him to come down to the strawberry patch with her to continue picking, and tried to explain to him that it wasn't usually so hot up here, that this was a heat wave, but she had the feeling he didn't believe her. It didn't really matter. He smiled and smiled at her.

She then proposed that they do a little watering. Everything was going to wilt if she didn't give things a good soaking. He agreed, and he helped her with the hoses and nozzles, and when the sprinkler was going birds came to flutter in the spray and to drink, and the thirsty garden drank, and Ann drank Abraham in, stealing a glance at him as she washed down the path that led to the house.

Then they sat up in the house, and shared a bowl of strawberries. He told her that they were his favorite food. He could almost live on strawberries alone. It was so hot by now that the earth was barely rotating. Ann proposed that they go out to the beach to cool off.

The air at the beach was quite a bit cooler, and Ann put a shirt on over her sundress, covering her back and shoulders. She hoped she hadn't appeared immodest to Abraham. He still hadn't touched her, but as they walked side by side along the water's edge their arms brushed once—and then again and again. Ann wasn't sure if it was an accident or if he was doing it or if she was. Finally, he proposed that they go sit up in the dunes.

There was an anxious expression on his face, and suddenly Ann was terrified that he had suddenly realized that he didn't like her. As soon as they sat down in the sand he began to tell her a tale of woe. He unburdened his heart to her and told her about the great problems of his life. She listened, sifting sand from one hand to the other. She wished that there were no sorrow in his life, especially since it was unnecessary. She happened to know the answer to his dilemma, and she explained it to him. He seemed a little taken aback, as if he wasn't used to the idea of problems having simple solutions and sorrow coming to an end.

As it was growing late, she proposed that they go back to the house. When they got there, however, it was hot as ever, so they brought the hose around to the back garden in hopes of reviving it. While they were watering they told each other about their past relationships. They had all been disasters.

"Have you ever seen a perfect relationship?" Ann asked.

"No," Abraham said. "But I still believe that one is possible."

"So do I," Ann said.

He followed her to the side of the house, because the side flower bed still needed to be wetted down, and while she was watering he put his arms around her and pulled her to him. Then the hose dropped from her hands and the water raced away and ran down the hill bringing relief at last to the aching thirsty world.

How He Was in Bed

THE PHONE RANG. It was Ann's friend, Leona. She wanted to come over.

"I've just fallen in love," Ann told her as soon as she walked in.

"Really?" Leona said. "So did I."

Ann was surprised, but delighted to hear it.

"Who is this guy?" Leona asked.

"His name is Abraham," Ann said. "He just left. He's been here the past three days. He had to go back down to the city. But who are *you* in love with?"

"Andrew Kelly. I've just been with him the last three days, also."

"That really is remarkable," Ann said. "Isn't love wonderful?" she asked.

"Shall we put on some music?" Leona asked.

"Turn it up," Leona said, starting to dance.

"I can't believe that life is so wonderful after all," Ann said, leaping and twirling.

"I'm so glad it happened to you, too, so you can understand how I feel," Ann said later, when Leona was getting ready to go. "But I thought Andrew was going with Mary."

"Not any more," Leona said. "He told me that she only likes it in the missionary position."

"The missionary position?" Ann asked. For a few moments she didn't know what Leona was talking about. Certainly this overwhelming love she felt for Abraham was not based on his interest in assuming a variety of coital positions. He was strong and tender, but their lovemaking had not been characterized by any special expertise. He loved her and she loved him. That was what made their lovemaking more exotic and thrilling than any she had ever experienced before.

The Practice Life

THE REASON, Abraham had said, that he had waited the whole day before touching Ann was this: he knew that what would then ensue would be the most important thing that had ever happened to him and he had wanted to be careful. That was why, also, he had made his confession in the dunes—so that Ann would know the worst about him first—to get that out of the way so that he wouldn't have to worry about her eventually discovering his terrible worry.

His terrible worry was this: He had been married before, just as Ann had been married before. He had a son, just as Ben had had a son. That son lived with his mother, but Abraham worried that his son was unhappy. His mother needed to go out a lot and the son was left home alone. Abraham worried that his son was lonely. His son was eleven, just the age little Bobby had been when he had come to live with Ann and Ben.

"Why don't you have him come and live with you?" Ann had suggested. She knew, from experience, that life was always richer with a child in the house. She loved Abraham for caring so deeply for his son. She wondered, however, at the coincidence. Was she going to live the same life twice?

Bobby had come to live with Ann and Ben and Ann had loved having him around. It had provided Ben with an excuse, however, for stepping out without her—someone had to stay home with Bobby. Ann had wondered, also, if Ben hadn't been jealous of her relationship with Bobby, and if that hadn't prompted him to have affairs. Ann wondered, finally, if Ben wasn't trying to compete with Bobby. After all, Bobby was just coming into his manhood. Ben's new girl friend was, indeed, much closer to Bobby's age than Ben's. Ann wondered if she and Ben would ever have broken up if Bobby hadn't come to live with them. And now she was advising the man with whom she hoped to become involved that he should have his son come live with him.

He seemed, indeed, surprised at her suggestion, as his previous girl friend had seen his son as an impediment.

But Ann wasn't Abraham's former girl friend and Abraham was not Ben. What had happened in the past didn't really matter. They had merely been practicing.

As If She Believed in God

ANN OPENED HER EYES. Abraham was sitting on the floor beside his bed on the floor where she lay watching him putting on his running shoes. Then he bent over her, kissed her, and sprinted out the door. She stretched and sat up. The morning sun had not yet broken through the fog. She pulled the blankets around her shoulders and looked around the room, blessing each object silently. Then she pulled on Abraham's robe and padded to the bathroom to start the water running for their bath.

She decided to make the bed this morning, to beat him at that task. As she pulled the covers from the mattress she thought to herself how incredible it was that Abraham was, in all respects, in every particular, down to the last detail, exactly as she would have him had she put an order in with God. As if she believed in God!

Suddenly she saw that the mattress they had been sleeping on was not really a mattress. It was a sofa cushion. It was much too narrow for even one person to sleep on comfortably. Yet they both had been sleeping on it very comfortably. It was impossible, and yet true. Just at that moment the fog lifted. The sun beamed in through the window and made a bright square on the floor.

The Marriage Made in Heaven

ANN DRESSED HERSELF all in white. She had attended to the animals and the garden, and now she could head down to Abraham's. The moon was just rising as she reached the highway. It was clear to her that she and Abraham couldn't go on the way they had been going—although it had only been for two weeks. It was too clumsy to have two houses.

She loved her house and had thought that she would die there. She loved the peace and privacy of living in the country. She loved the pure sweet air, she loved to pick her fruit from the trees, and she loved to watch the sequence of flowers appear and disappear each year. Her house was more than a house. It had watched her life unfold. She was finally living in that house the way it wanted to be lived in and the heart of the house had opened. That house had become the world to her.

Now, Ann saw, it was nothing. She would gladly give it up and go to live with Abraham, even in the city.

She parked the car in front of his gate and quickly walked up the path to his cottage. Suddenly she was inside and his arms were around her. Some music was playing. Angels seemed to be singing.

Then he told her what he had been thinking. The separation was too painful.

"Yes," Ann said. She had been thinking the same. She would move to the city.

"I want you to marry me," Abraham said.

"Yes," Ann said. Although she had sworn many times she would never marry again. But this would be different. This would be a marriage made in heaven. And the angels sang their affirmation.

The Angel Drove a Bus

IT JUST SO HAPPENED that that weekend Ann's father was going to be in the city on business.

"I'd like you to meet him," Ann had said.

"I'd like very much to meet him," Abraham had said. And Ann had smiled, happy that Abraham wished to show respect to her father. Now there was even more reason for them to meet. For now he was her fiancé.

She went alone in the morning and had breakfast with her father before his business meeting. Then, when they had comfortably settled into their booth, she told him that she had met a man two weeks ago and they had fallen in love. He was a good man, and last night he had asked her to marry him. Now they were engaged. She would like them to meet.

Her father smiled. Ann wasn't sure that he believed her.

So she was a bit nervous as she and Abraham walked towards her father's hotel that night. She wanted her father to like Abraham and she wanted Abraham to like her father. Just then, a bus rumbled by splashing oil up at them. Ann jumped, but Abraham was not so fast. There was oil all over his shoes.

Then suddenly a shoeshine stand appeared, right before the entrance to the hotel. Abraham climbed up and offered his feet.

All this happened in a little less than five minutes, and they were still on time for their appointment with Ann's father.

The three of them went into dinner, and after it was over the waiter brought Ann's father the bill. Abraham tried to take it, but Ann's father insisted. He would pay. The waiter returned to see if he was ready to pay. Then Ann's father pointed out that the bill was incorrect. The waiter had charged him too little. Ann was glad of this opportunity for Abraham to glimpse her father's integrity.

Abraham went to get their coats. Then Ann asked her father what he thought of Abraham. He told her he was very favorably impressed. He could tell from even this short meeting that Abraham was a very fine person. He was very polite and his shoes were shined.

The Nightmare

ANN NEVER SAW BEN. She never had anything to do with him. As far as she was concerned, that was a closed book. She didn't even have a picture of him. That period of her life was over. Abraham was her world now. For the first time in her life she felt totally loved. She felt she had permission, at last, to be herself. She was totally secure, never afraid that Abraham would hurt her, that she would displease him, that he would grow tired of her, that he would see through her. He saw her as she was—with all her perfections and imperfections, and he loved it all. He always gave her pleasure. They often thought the same thoughts and could talk without speaking. They had known each other only a short time, but it felt like forever, as if they had been together in all eternity.

Then Ben began to visit Ann in her dreams. He pleaded with her to return to him, to help him, to take care of him. He needed her. She awoke with a shudder.

Then Abraham held her to him. And he explained to her that marriage was forever.

The Baby Laughs

ONCE UPON A TIME there was a little baby waiting on the moon to be born. For a long time it had been watching Ann. It watched Ann and Ben and sighed, for there was not enough love there to bring this babe to earth. And it watched as Ben went away and Ann went about her business, and it drummed its little fingers on the cold surface of the moon, for it was growing impatient.

It had also been watching Abraham. It saw Abraham when he told his girl friend that he didn't want to have any more babies, and it had seen his girl friend say that then he didn't really love her, for if he really loved her he would want to have her baby, and the baby nodded its little head in agreement, for it was made entirely of love, and it knew that this was so. And it watched that woman disappear and Abraham sit alone in his house, unaware that he was being watched.

Then one night when Ann and Abraham had almost despaired of finding true love, God brought them together. Then the babe knew that it wouldn't be long now, and the moon shone a little brighter, for, although many people think that the moon gets its light from reflection, it is love which is the source of all light. And the baby laughed.

Meanwhile, Back on Earth

MEANWHILE, back on earth, Abraham was cooking breakfast for Ann. "Say," he said to her as he stirred the eggs, "I've been meaning to ask you. What type of birth control do you use?"

"I use the ovulation method," Ann said.

"The what?" Abraham asked.

"The ovulation method. I figure out when I'm ovulating. A woman is only fertile a few days a month. There's no point in using dangerous drugs or torture devices for the whole month when a woman is only fertile a few days. So I abstain or use a condom when I'm fertile."

"I knew a woman who did it that way. By the phases of the moon. And *she* got pregnant," Abraham said. The toast was starting to burn.

"Well, I don't do it by the moon," Ann said. I check my temperature and mucus," Ann said. "It's very scientific."

"Well, what if you *do* get pregnant?" Abraham said, taking her in his arms. "That wouldn't be so bad. In fact, it would be wonderful. A little Ann! I can't believe I'm saying this. I never thought I'd feel this way."

"Yes, it *would* be wonderful," Ann said. She couldn't believe he was saying this. She never thought anyone would ever say this to her. "But I don't even know if I can get pregnant," she said. "I've never been pregnant."

"That's the silliest thing I ever heard," Abraham said. "You're the most fertile person I've ever met."

"Do you really think so?" Ann asked.

"Yes, I do," Abraham said. "And I love you. And I want to have your baby."

"Well, we can't try until we're married," Ann said. "I don't even know if I can get pregnant."

"Just give me a chance," the baby said.

What Happens to the Hurt

"DO YOU KNOW what I was just thinking?" Abraham asked as they drove along. "I was thinking that I'll never sleep with another woman."

"Oh," Ann said. Of course, she thought, she would now never sleep with another man. There was nothing of sacrifice in that thought, or of wistfulness. She had seen enough of the rest of the world not to lust after it. But then, monogamy was easy for her, as she was a woman. For Ben, monogamy had been too great a sacrifice, too restricting. He was not going to live forever, and he didn't want to miss anything from life.

"Not that I won't occasionally feel attracted to other women. I'm sure I will," Abraham said. She never would have demanded this commitment from Abraham. She knew that there is no commitment when it's demanded. She didn't even know if, in this day and age, such commitment was appropriate. She had felt guilty when she had felt hurt by Ben.

"I never want to hurt you," Abraham said.

"And I never want to hurt you," Ann said. How lucky she and Abraham were, she thought, for they had never hurt each other. For, she knew, if people hurt each other they can apologize and forgive each other and discuss it for long hours into the night, but it never really goes away.

Who Should Worry

IT HAD BEEN DIFFICULT, but at last Ann and Abraham had been able to convince Tina, his son William's mother, to allow him to come and live with them for a while. Now Ann was worried that William would never warm to her. She knew she couldn't expect to replace Tina in his affections. She had never tried to replace Bobby's mother, Beth. Beth was a good person. Tina, also, seemed to be a very good person. They were all good people and yet all these homes were broken. Ann sighed. This new world was full of fragmented families and what could be done about it? Ann could never be for these children what their real parents were. Then what had she been for Bobby? A friend, perhaps. Suddenly she was flooded with memories of her life with Bobby and Ben. She remembered sewing by the fire while Ben read a story to Bobby. She remembered Ben playing ball with Bobby and Ben going over Bobby's homework with him, their blond heads bent together over Bobby's books. However dissolvable Ann and Ben's relationship had been there was nothing that could alter the tie that bound Ben and Bobby. They were father and son; they loved each other. So Abraham and William were father and son and so they loved each other. Ann knew that William must be worrying about where he would fit into the new family they were creating. Ann hoped that she would be able to help him to feel secure. She was the one who should worry.

What People Will Believe

ANN AND ABRAHAM'S FRIENDS were very glad, though surprised, to hear that Ann and Abraham had suddenly fallen in love. That was great, only, they wanted to know, were they joking? Was it a hoax? A practical joke? They hadn't known Ann and Abraham to play jokes before. It was spendid news, Ann and Abraham's friends said; they just wondered why they hadn't been consulted. It was super, but when were Ann and Abraham going to have their first fight? When they had their first fight Ann and Abraham's friends would begin to take their relationship seriously. They would be there to advise and nurse them through the crises. They could be counted on. They knew someone who was very good at couples' counseling. As soon as Ann and Abraham started "working" on their relationship, then their friends would begin to take it seriously. As soon as Ann and Abraham stopped being so happy they would believe in it.

The Little Annoyances

BEN CAME TO ANN in her dreams and pleaded with her to come back to him. He was sick and he was lonely. He appealed to her compassion. He was sorry for the way he had treated her; he had changed; he was different now. She was the one he really loved.

Ann felt sorry for him. She didn't want to hurt him anymore by saying, "I don't love you, I love Abraham." But she was annoyed with him for bothering her in her dreams again. Even if there were significant changes in his character, would it matter? It was all the little things about him which she couldn't stand.

"But Ben," she said, "you and I always annoyed each other. Abraham and I don't annoy each other. That's the difference."

An Angel Comes to Call Off the Sacrifice

THE COTTAGE Abraham was renting in the city was too small for the three of them, so Ann and Abraham were looking for another house. The real estate agent was not optimistic. The houses available were both expensive and depressing. After living in the country, where she didn't have curtains on her windows and couldn't see her neighbors, it shocked Ann to look out of city windows at other city windows with their blinds drawn tight. But Ann wasn't worried. She knew something suitable would turn up. She and Abraham were lucky.

The real estate agent, however, was worried. And Abraham was worried. School started for William in a few short weeks. They would have to be settled by then.

They spent the weekend at Ann's house in the country. William had wanted to go. He loved it there. In the city, he never played outside. Here he liked to range in the orchard.

Ann, also, was glad to be home. In a few weeks she would have to say goodby to her house forever. She and Abraham would live in the city and her house would be sold so that Ben could have his half of the value.

Ann was happy to be home, but she was worried about Abraham because he was worried. "Don't worry, dear," he said. "Sometimes it seems like something terrible is happening and it turns out later to be a great thing instead. I'm miserable and frightened, but I have the feeling that this is one of those times."

They looked at each other. Suddenly it dawned on them that they could stay there. *They* could buy Ben's half of the house and stay in the country. But only if William were willing to leave the city. It all depended on William.

As it happened, William was eager to live in the country. Everything was working perfectly. Abraham, also, was eager to live in the country, though he had been willing to stay in the city because he thought William wanted to and, moreover, because he thought Ann wanted to. But she had only been willing to move to the city because she thought William and Abraham wanted to stay there. Now they could all three get their wish. But there was one fly in the ointment: William's mother, Tina. She would never go for it.

And, indeed, William's mother, Tina, did not like the idea of William going to live in the country. How could she? But of course, all that country air would be good for him. Of course, William could visit her on weekends. The time they spent together would be quality, not quantity. Tina would eventually agree. This plan was best for everyone. But surely somebody would have to feel guilty.

Abraham Tells Ann He Loves Her

MANY TIMES A DAY Abraham would take Ann in his arms and hug her and kiss her and tell her he loved her. If he left the house for even a few minutes he would kiss her and tell her he loved her. He didn't need to tell her. She knew that he loved her. But the telling was a pleasure. And every day, also, he told her she was beautiful, and when he did she would go and sit in his lap and he would kiss her and tell her he loved her, and she told him she loved him again and again, for her love for him was always welling up and overflowing, and it was a pleasure to be able always to tell him, without embarrassment, how she loved him, without restraint, she loved him, without fear that her love wouldn't be returned. It *was* returned, over and over, and she never got tired of hearing it.

The Glass Is Broken

THE WEDDING GUESTS began to arrive. Friends and relations. The dead and dying. The cynical. The beaten. The lost. Those who lusted after power. Those who lusted after success. Those whose love had dried to dust. And they gathered from far and near. Even though the storm had begun to roar. The storm which was their lives began to toss. And it blew all about the house. And torrents of rain poured forth while inside all was aglow. All was aglow in the flickering firelight. Under the marriage canopy all was at peace. There Ann and Abraham joined hands, their little dog at their feet. Then William handed Abraham the ring, and Ann and Abraham promised to love each other forever and ever. Everyone looked on, but they just saw each other. And the glass was broken.

What the Storm Brewed

RICE RAINED DOWN through the rain as Ann and Abraham ran to the car. At last they were alone together. They headed west, holding hands inside the storm. The rain washed down, carrying with it the seeds of every living thing. Trees bowed down as they passed and the grasses began to grow, and as they drove all the hills grew greener and greener until they reached the sea. Then Abraham turned the car up a side road and they reached the inn where a room was waiting for them. Inside, a fire had been laid, and they quickly lit it, then sat down on the rug before it to warm themselves. While they watched, the fire burned red and orange and gold and blue and green. Outside the window, the storm beat rhythmically, returning to the ocean which beat against the shore. Abraham took Ann in his arms. And so their union was consecrated.

Ann slept. Meanwhile, up on the moon, Baby Lena was watching. She saw Ann and Abraham driving down a dusty road in an old pick-up truck. She heard them singing:

"Oh we ain't got a barrel of money
Maybe we're ragged and funny
But we'll travel along
Singin' our song
Side by side

"Oh we don't know what's comin' tomorrow
Maybe it's trouble and sorrow
But we'll travel the road
Carryin' our load
Side by side

"Through all kinds of weather
What if the sky should fall?
Well as long as we're together
It really doesn't matter at all

"When they've all had their troubles and parted
We'll be the same as we started
We'll just travel along
Singin' our song—"

They brought the truck to a halt. Someone was waiting on the road, thumb out.

"Can you give me a ride?" Baby Lena asked. "I'm an orphan—I have no parents. And I haven't got a vehicle—no way to get about."

"Please, climb aboard," Ann and Abraham said, and the three of them set off again. Now three of them were singing.

The Great Lady

ANN AND ABRAHAM walked on the beach. The storm had vanished and the world was new.

"What do you think of the name 'Lena'?" Ann asked.

"I like it," Abraham said. "Why?"

"Well, I just thought that if we should ever have a baby—not that I think I could ever get pregnant—and it should be a girl, then we should name her Lena. I don't know why. The name just came into my head. I don't have any associations with it."

"I do," Abraham said. "My great grandmother was named Lena."

"What was she like?" Ann asked. The ocean at her feet was vast and deep.

"She was a great lady," Abraham said.

Spring Cleaning

ONE DAY when Ann was circumambulating the house she noticed that some bushes that Ben had planted long ago and which had looked stunted and had always refused to grow were suddenly large, large and flowering. They were beautiful, healthy bushes, and they graced the slope on which they stood. Ann was surprised. And she thought with pity how Ben never got to enjoy the fruits of his labors. And she was surprised at her pity.

She had forgotten everything good about Ben. Now sweet memories of their life together began to surface. The many walks they had taken together. The many letters he had written her—long ago, when he had first met her and she had gone home to her parents in the summer.

That night she lay awake while her mind wandered down the hall and into the cupboard and rifled through the letters

Ben had written her. For a long time, she had wanted to throw these letters away, but she had not yet been able to. But now that she had finally loosened the bonds of hatred she could deal with them. She would put them in the attic.

The Source of the Emotions

ANN WAS ON HER WAY HOME when suddenly she decided to stop at the delicatessen. There she bought a couple of big juicy sour pickles. They would go well with tonight's dinner. By the time she got home she had eaten them both.

Abraham was listening to a ball game. She went and sat on his lap and watched the sun go down. Suddenly she was crying.

He was very tender. He had not seen her cry many times before. She told him she was thinking about her parents and how much she loved them. She was worried that they didn't see how much she cared for them.

"I'm sure they do, and I'm sure they love you, too, just as much," Abraham said.

"Well, that isn't really it," Ann said. "That isn't what's making me sad."

"What is it, then?" Abraham asked.

"I'm sad because I can never get pregnant," Ann blubbered.

Abraham smiled at her. "Why are you smiling?" Ann asked through her tears.

"Because I think you're pregnant *now*," Abraham said.

"No I'm not," Ann said. "It's just that I'm expecting my period and it's late. That's why I'm so emotional."

The Perfect Circle

ABRAHAM BROUGHT HOME a home pregnancy test kit from the drugstore and Ann added her first morning's midstream urine to the chemicals. Now they had to leave the test tube undisturbed for two hours. They went outside, even though it was raining lightly. Ann walked around nervously and told Abraham over and over that it was probably a waste of money. She was sure she wasn't pregnant. She believed fervently in the power of negative thinking, and this was her way of praying.

Abraham just smiled and agreed that the test probably was unnecessary. He didn't need it to show him that Ann was pregnant. He was sure she was pregnant.

So the two hours passed and finally they dared to sneak up on the test which would show a random pattern if she wasn't pregnant and a complete circle if she was.

There it was. A perfect circle.

They held each other tight. They were too happy to speak.

They decided to take a drive to celebrate. They drove towards the redwoods and the Russian River. Yesterday's storm was being pushed out of the sky by today's. The sun dashed in and out of the clouds. The world was alive, wet, and green.

All week long the river had been rising. Now as they turned onto River Road they saw that this placid little river where they had swum in the summer was now huge—swollen and churning, carrying everything with it in its path. It almost reached them on the road, and they turned and followed it as it turned and raced away in its undeniable inevitable surge to the sea.

The Origin of the Will

ANN WAS HAVING TROUBLE waking up in the morning. She slept late almost every day, and Abraham let her sleep, closing the bedroom door so that she wouldn't be disturbed. She was no sooner up and dressed than she felt sleepy again and lay down again for a midmorning nap. In the afternoons, also, though she tried to stay alert, she found herself drifting and dozing, and then dreaming. Each night she went to bed early, and she dreamed beautiful vivid dreams, elegant architectural dreams unlike any she had ever dreamed. Try as she might, she couldn't stop sleeping, for Baby Lena wanted her asleep, needed her to dream. It was when Ann was asleep that the embryo that Baby Lena was was able to grow. Baby Lena flourished there in Ann's unconscious. She willed Ann unconscious. And it was from Ann's unconscious that she exercised her will.

The Impossible Distance

ANN WAS LOOKING OUT THE WINDOW. Abraham was at work, William was at his grandparents'. She was alone in the house. But was she alone? Someone else was there, inside her. Someone was there, closer than close, yet it was someone she couldn't see.

Ann was wearing glasses. She had had to give up her contact lenses for the duration of her pregnancy. The shape of her eyeballs had changed. She resented her glasses. They came between her and the world. She sat behind her glasses behind the window.

Outside the window the sun was shining on the trees and grasses and bright red berries. The breeze seemed to inspire the branches of the camellia which thrilled with pink blossom. But Ann was behind the window, in the dark inside the window, and the window showed her that the world existed and then imposed an impossible distance.

As She Sang

ANN HAD A BOOK of photographs of the development of the embryo. It was a blind worm, then a sea horse, then a frog. It had no hands, then it had paddles. It floated in its watery world in ecstasy. Ann felt nauseated. She sipped apricot nectar and nibbled on toast. She lay on the couch. Quickly the embryo developed. At last it turned into a fetus—a little human with a large round head. Ann got up from the couch and went outside. Her baby now had eyes and ears. It could see the golden glow of sunlight shining through her skin, and it listened as she sang.

How She Looked

WHEN ANN AND BEN first broke up people frequently remarked on how beautiful and how young Ann now looked. She thought perhaps that people were trying to comfort her, but then she saw that probably there was some truth in it. After all, she was less tired now that she didn't have to carry Ben around her neck. She no longer clenched her jaw. Now she walked around with her eyes wide open. Now her head turned from side to side. Now she moved freely through the world.

Abraham, of course, thought her very beautiful and told her so constantly. But he was in love with her and love was, after all, blind. But he told her so often that she almost believed him.

Now that she was pregnant more people than ever were telling her she was beautiful. But of course pregnant women often look beautiful. They are full of life.

Still Ann wondered about these comments. She knew that in reality everything about her was quite ordinary. Everything but her happiness.

The Simple Truth

ANN AND BEN had run into each other.

"The problem with our relationship was that you didn't love me," Ann said. "If you had loved me, you wouldn't have treated me the way you did."

"That isn't exactly true," Ben said. "When I lied to you I was lying to myself."

"And I didn't love you purely, either," Ann said. "I was in love with your position, your prestige. I couldn't admit I had made a mistake. We never should have married."

"But our marriage *was* something," Ben said. "It was something."

"Our story is totally ordinary," Ann said. "I'm sure it's no different from a lot of people's stories," Ann said.

"But *we* weren't ordinary," Ben said. "We were so clever at it. Look at how long it went on!"

"I don't think that's so clever," Ann said. "Anyway, some people go on a lot longer, poor souls."

"The trouble with you is that you think things are simple," Ben said.

"Things *are* simple," Ann said.

The Labor of Love

THE ROOM which Ann made into a baby room was obviously an addition to the original house. There was a window between it and Ann and Abraham's bedroom. On the window Ann had hung a beautiful patchwork quilt as a curtain.

It had been given to her by Elizabeth, her friend John's ex-wife, before she had left him, before Ben had left her, many years ago, when they had all been friends. It had been ragged when Elizabeth had given it to her, but she had shown Ann how the torn patches could be replaced, though she herself had never made the effort to do it.

Ann, also, never worked on it. Then one day Ben's father and stepmother had come from very far to visit. They had sat outside at the picnic table sewing haphazardly on the quilt while Ben cowered in the house. Ann had tried to patch up the relationship between Ben and his father, but all she could do was a haphazard job. The quilt wasn't really patched properly then, but it had seemed better, and Ann had put it on their bed where the dog jumped up with his sharp claws and ripped it further to shreds.

After all, it was old, incredibly old, and whoever had originally conceived of it had worked at it with faithful devotion. But somewhere over the years that faith had been broken. Now Ann began to mend it.

The Nature of Miracles

ANN WAS SURPRISED when she saw other women who were pregnant. They couldn't be as pregnant as she was, she thought to herself. She was surprised, also, when she noticed the cows in the fields down the road. Each one had a calf! And the sheep—each ewe had a lamb. Each goat had a kid! How could this be?, Ann wondered, for she knew there had never been anything more amazing, more beautiful or more miraculous than her own pregnancy.

Ann Chooses Life in Spite of the Financial Setback

"HOW YA DOIN'?" Chet, one of Ann's colleagues at work, asked her.

"Really well," Ann said. "Now that I'm over my morning sickness. I'm pregnant, you know."

"*Good* luck!" Chet said, pulling out his cigaretts. "Seems like my wife and I are the last couple on earth who aren't having kids."

Ann was surprised to hear that he was married. He had always tried to flirt with her. "Don't you want kids?" she asked.

"No way!" Chet said. "Do you know how much it costs to raise a kid? $85,000! I could have a boat!"

Ann wondered if he would ever actually have a boat. "Doesn't your wife want a baby?" she asked.

"Luckily, she doesn't," Chet said. "She teaches nursery school and has to put up with kids all day at work. Actually, she loves her work, but she likes to relax when she comes home."

Ann wondered if Mrs. Chet really wanted a boat as much as Chet did, or if she was just trying to please Chet.

"Believe me," Chet said, "we thought it all through and we made our choice." And he lit his cigarette.

As Perfect as She Was

WHEN ANN CONTEMPLATED having a child with Ben the thought always came to her that his child would probably be a freak. Not that freaks ran in her family, but Ann secretly believed that she herself was a freak—otherwise, why was she treated like one? Ben was very squeamish. It was clear to her what would have happened had their love produced a physical embodiment—she would have been left alone to contend with it.

Nonetheless, Ann did not believe that the baby now growing inside of her was in any way a freak. And what if it was? Then she and Abraham would love it nonetheless. Still, she felt enough loyalty to her old habits of thought to express her concern to Abraham. She liked to hear him laugh at her doubts. He knew their baby was perfect—as perfect as she was.

It Grows Larger

ANN AND EVE and Kick Me were traveling in a small boat. Adam and Eve jumped out, and who was left? Just then Baby Lena gave Ann a big kick. Ann put Abraham's hand on her belly. They smiled at each other. A lump appeared and then was retracted. An elbow? Baby Lena was trying out her wings. Abraham stroked Ann's belly. Abraham stroked Ann's thigh. How could it be that their love, already so full, kept growing larger?

How She Found Herself

THERE HAD BEEN SO many lies between Ann and Ben that though they had lived side by side they had really been miles apart. But there were no lies between Ann and Abraham. Not the smallest lie. Not the whitest lie. One lie leads to another and another and another. If Ann had a funny feeling she always told him. She didn't have to protect herself from Abraham's anger. She didn't have to protect him from all bother and worry. She didn't have to carry a load of guilt and resentment locked in her heart. She loved to confess to Abraham everything she was feeling, thinking. Telling him what was on her mind helped her to see what was on her mind. It was, to her, a sumptuous luxury never to have to hide. Because she didn't have to hide from Abraham she didn't have to hide from herself. That was how she found herself.

The Door Opens

HOW HAD ALL THE THOUSANDS, the millions of women all through the ages suffered this, Ann wondered as each contraction gripped her. She had been in labor for nineteen hours. Abraham had never left her side, and he had suffered each contraction with her. In the labor rooms next to them they could hear women screaming. Why hadn't anyone prepared them? Ann didn't scream. She needed every ounce of energy to focus on her breathing, to focus on her belly, to open the door—and who would enter? Suddenly, she felt an overwhelming urge to push. Finally they were wheeling her to the delivery room. There the lights dimmed. People spoke in hushed voices. Someone was whispering in her ear—it was a woman's voice. She could see her baby's hairy head now in the mirror—larger with each push. She saw Abraham in a hat and mask pulling on gloves. "Now!" the voice whispered, and her baby came rushing out into the world.

It's a Boy!

ABRAHAM CAUGHT THE BABY as it appeared. Then Ann reached down to pull it onto her belly. The baby had a look of utter determination on its face. It was covered with the greasy white vernix which had protected it in the womb. Someone covered it with a blanket. Ann held it to her. A minute ago she had been utterly exhausted, now she was ready to do it all again. The cord now had stopped throbbing. Abraham cut it. The doctor was examining the placenta. All the colors in the room were blue and red. Ann put the baby to her breast where it began to nurse. She had hardly looked at it, but she knew it was perfect. "Don't you want to know if it's a boy or girl?" the doctor asked. "Why don't you look under the blanket?" the doctor suggested. So Abraham looked under the blanket. "It's a boy," he said. Ann could hear the disappointment in his voice.

Hello, Lena

"I THINK YOU BETTER LOOK a little higher," the doctor said. "Oh! It's a girl!" Abraham said. He had not realized that the genitals of a newborn are swollen. "Hello, Lena," Ann said. Outside in the world the sun was just setting. Birds flew through the sky. The wind rustled in the trees.